KINGFISHER LANE

By Grant Gosch

Copyright © 2022 Grant Gosch.

All rights reserved. No part of this publication may be reproduced, distributed, or transmitted in any form or by any means, including photocopying, recording, or other electronic or mechanical methods, without the prior written permission of the publisher, except in the case of brief quotations embodied in critical reviews and certain other noncommercial uses permitted by copyright law. For permission requests, write to the publisher, addressed "Attention: Permissions Coordinator," at the address below.

ISBN: 979-8-9870279-1-2

Any references to historical events, real people, or real places are used fictitiously. Names, characters, and places are products of the author's imagination.

Kingfisher Lane
Cover painting: Stella Hanamori
Cover layout: Jon Minor
Editing: Kyra Wojdyla, Kristin Widing, Ann Gosch

First printing edition 2022.

Ocean Creek Publishing

www.grantgosch.com

Grant Gosch   Kingfisher Lane

I dedicate this book to the women in my life.
I would be a bedraggled pile of mess without you.

Henry

I have stayed in bed the last three mornings and watched the kingfisher. His brilliant blue-tufted head motionless, his eyes fixed on the tide pool below. The driftwood snag he sits on has been locked in sand and mud for a week. The snag floated into my cove during the last king tide and settled itself on the beach in front of my cabin—a migratory piece of wood finding rest until the next full moon unroots it and sends it farther down the Salish Sea. The kingfisher is poised to strike, aiming his spear-like bill a millimeter up, a millimeter down, left, right, as he runs through a list of prehistoric equations accounting for water depth, wind speed, and light refraction. I've watched him plunge into the tide pool five times this morning, and each time he returns to his perch with a writhing sculpin. He never misses.

When I focus on small things, I don't think about her. This morning, just like the last three, it's been the kingfisher. I'll watch him until he's full of tiny fish or until the tide rises high enough to return his hunting ground and its aquatic captives back into the flow of Emerald Pass. When he flies away, my friend the kingfisher, I will walk to the piano and play the song I wrote all those years ago. The song I wrote for her.

I will stay at the piano until the alpenglow loses its grip on the Olympic Mountains. Then I'll walk to the front door of my cabin, slip on my rubber boots, and hike the five switchbacks to Kingfisher Lane with Oscar, my spaniel mutt. Today I will try to find enough blackberries for a pie. It's late in the season, but the shade berries are still plump and full of flavor.

I promised Thelma I would bring a pie to the potluck in the old barn at the headwaters of Oyster Creek. The Performing Arts Center, we like to call it. Thelma is old, Thelma is kind, I don't want to disappoint Thelma. So, pie, then. Pie is what I will do after watching the kingfisher, after the piano, after the walk with Oscar up the five switchbacks and down the lane. Then I will make pie. That will be nice. Pie.

This is how things go for me. One observation, one song, one walk, one pie, one day after the next. It's a good life, I think. But underneath it all is the story of her. Underneath it all is a love that still finds me in my dreams. It catches me off guard. It makes me ache. I feel foolish, sometimes, loving like this. But it's not a choice.

After watching the kingfisher, I walk to the front door and Oscar, sensing the time is at hand for our morning adventure, bolts past my legs and noses open the bottom of the Dutch door, leaving it a spaniel's width ajar. He darts up the fern-lined trail and crosses the footbridge that spans Oyster Creek. Instead of taking the switchbacks, he cuts straight through the woods and up to Kingfisher Lane. I don't stop him. Cars seldom come down this way, and if they did, we would hear them a long way off, transmissions whining in protest as they downshift on the descent into my cove. There are no sounds from cars today.

Oscar is in the woods across the lane when I crest the trail. I always know where he is. Spaniels are bred to flush birds, and Oscar has taken his genetic code to heart. He's only thirty-five pounds but he sounds like a grizzly sow romping through the underbrush when he runs off-trail. There are no quail on this part of the island, so Oscar takes to flushing jays and robins.

Once, he spooked a sleeping deer and her fawn from where they nestled down near Kingfisher Lane. That was a proud moment for Oscar, spooking an animal ten times his size. After he flushed the deer, he wiggled his nub-tailed ass like it had a mind of its own. I don't like him disturbing the wild things, but the pride in his hopeful brown eyes was too much for me. I couldn't help but lean down and give him a scratch behind the ear.

Sometimes I see him sitting on the porch looking off toward the setting sun with a wistful expression, like a war veteran remembering his moment of valor. The way he holds his snout, at an upward angle, lets me know he's thinking about how he flushed those deer. It might have been the proudest moment of his life.

I walk in the middle of the road and make my way to the blackberry bushes that mark the end of Kingfisher Lane. It's late fall and the road is littered with alder and maple leaves. I only step on the yellow leaves. Not the red ones. Not the green ones. Just the yellow ones. The yellow leaves are typically close together but sometimes I need to jump four feet to get to the next leaf. That's how the game works. That's how she taught me to play—only the yellow leaves. So, as best I can, I jump.

How odd this must look. An old man jumping from yellow leaf to yellow leaf on an empty lane while a spaniel mutt runs wild from one side of the road to the other, barking with joy and crashing into the forest. What a pair we are. Silly dog. Silly man. Silly life.

When my attention is not focused on the next yellow leaf, I think about the walk Rose and I took down the lane all those years ago. The feather that floated down from the canopy and landed in her dark hair. The alder sapling that brushed my leg when I kissed her for the last time.

ROSE

Rose stood on the passenger deck of the ferry and watched Alder Island reveal itself through the fog. Her hair, shoulder-length, black with stray grays, feathered over her face like a luffing sail. She reached into her pocket, found a hairband, piled her hair into a low bun, then gripped the handrail that ran along the passenger deck. She leaned out over the water and watched the gray bow waves splash against the green hull of the boat. Rose ran her thumbs over the chipped paint of the handrail and took in the details of its cracks and dents. She thought of all the hands that had gripped the rail over the years, looking for reassurance on their way to adventure, escape, or homecoming.

Rose looked at her own hands, the veins having retreated from the cool air, and thought about all that her hands had felt since they last felt Henry. Handshakes, home loans, divorce papers. *Will he recognize these hands? Will he see how much a part of me he has become? Yes, yes, I think he will.* Rose pulled her gaze up and caught the eye of a gull. The bird hung in a pocket of air above the ferry, catching a ride to the island. Rose's eyes fixed on the red blotch on its lower bill as the bird glided without effort, cocking its head from side to side. *I wonder what that would be like*, she thought, *floating on air looking down at the world*. Then, noticing her attention, the gull edged its wings, caught the wind, and swooped back out of sight.

Twelve years had passed since Rose last stood on the ferry's deck, heading in the opposite direction, away from the island, her younger hands holding on to the rail. She remembered what it felt like all those years ago. She remembered driving off the ferry and onto the mainland feeling like she was leaving home. It felt wrong. It felt backward. The world seemed looser, less attached to what she thought she knew. And then, in the grip of responsibility and maternal love, she drove east to Spokane. Back to Simon and the kids. Back to the comfort she had worked so hard to curate for the ones who meant the most in her life.

Rose remembered every detail of her time on the island with Henry. She replayed it in her mind while driving carpool, while sitting through gallery board meetings, and almost every night as she searched for sleep. And, although she was loath to admit it, the memories found her when she made love to Simon.

 Rose looked out over the slate gray water and recited aloud the line of a Mary Oliver poem that changed her life. "One day you finally knew what you had to do, and began." She was tired of being alone in Simon's company. She was tired of living life adjacent. It was time to begin. Again.

Henry

Before the walk down the lane, before the kingfisher on the snag, before Rose, there was the leaving-dream. It came to Henry like an approaching thunderstorm. Claps of sound. Images cast in brilliant light. Each one closer than the last.

Flash.

The island.

Boom.

The sea.

In his dream, Henry saw himself driving north on I-5. He saw himself returning to Washington State and the old cabin on Alder Island. When he woke, Henry reached for his journal on the nightstand and flipped to the page marked by an owl feather. He ran his thumb over the crisp white paper, and then, with the warm Santa Ana wind blowing waves in the curtains, he wrote the words: Goodbye, LA.

Henry had moved to Los Angeles by following a dream just as profound as the one that told him to leave. After graduating high school, Henry followed the flight path for boys his age. He worked the summer in the strawberry fields sixty miles north of his family home in Seattle. And then, that fall, Henry's mother waved him goodbye in front of the freshman dorm at the University of Washington.

"I'll pick up your laundry next week!" his mother said after hugging him. Then she took a step back and looked up at her son. "You have a dreamer's heart, Henry David James. Listen to what it tells you." She kissed his cheek, then narrowed her eyes. "Be true to yourself, Henry."

And then, that first night in the dorm, Henry dreamt of LA. He saw himself in the shadows of the Hollywood Hills, elbow to elbow with screenwriters and wannabe actors. He saw himself writing the songs that came to him in his dreams.

Henry's first class, Introduction to Psychology, started at 9:00 a.m. the following day. With books in hand, he walked across the quad in a sea of migrating students as rain beaded up on his twill jacket. When he arrived in front of the ivy-draped building that housed the psychology department, he put his hand on the rail that led up the stairs and to the front doors of the building while students streamed by him like wave wash. The handrail anchored him. He was held fast. It would not let him go. When at last he loosened his grip, his heart had made a decision. He turned, walked back to his dorm, packed his backpack, took the number sixteen bus to downtown Seattle and boarded a Greyhound for LA.

Rose

Fly like wild
Fly like wild
Fly away from here

As a child, Rose would slip away in the afternoons and dance in the woods behind her house. She would twirl her body through the ponderosa pines and juniper, her feet kicking up the smell of the desert. She would leap from rock to rock and spread her arms wide, pretending to fly through the wild world.

Growing up in Spokane was like living in a nest at the top of a tree; if she was going to leave, she would need to grow wings. And on the day after her high school graduation, despite her parents' apprehension, Rose unfolded her wings and flew to Italy.

She found work at a cafe in Rome serving cappuccinos to English-speaking tourists and in the evenings she would take long walks along the *Foro Romano* with her sketchbook in hand. Mopeds and Fiats would zip by while she sketched the form and angles of granite and travertine ruins. She would take rubbings of ancient blocks, creating impressions of history that she would pin up in her apartment.

As the year wore on, Rose began adding paint to her sketches and she became enamored with color and light. She spent a whole day on the steps of the Colosseum with one of her paintings, marveling at how the color changed as the sun edged across the sky.

When she returned home from her travels, she compiled her sketches and sent them along with an application to the Gonzaga University art program. She was accepted with a generous scholarship and jumped into her studies with the same enthusiasm she had employed when dancing through the woods as a child.

One spring morning, she found an unlocked door at the campus gallery. She slipped in, closed the door behind her, put on her headphones, and danced through the gallery as the morning light illuminated the art on the walls into a mosaic of color and feeling. It was a transcendent moment for Rose, and she felt wildly alive. *Art, light, and dance. My recipe for a well-lived life*, she thought.

Henry

After a year of working construction during the day and writing songs at night, Henry experienced a small measure of success when three of his songs were used by a UCLA film-school student in her senior project. The review in the school newspaper stated simply that the film was horrible and the only thing that kept people in their seats was the music. One of the reviewing professors passed Henry's name to an independent filmmaker, and soon he was writing soundtracks for low-budget movies.

Henry spent his twenties in LA writing songs in coffee shops and dive bars. He preferred the dive bars. He could see a song inside each person that walked through the doors—melodies of addiction, choruses of tragedy. Henry would sing their songs under his breath as he watched them sip their drinks and scan the room for a matching set of lonely eyes.

> I don't know him anymore
> The child of my youth
> I don't know him anymore
> Sweet boy

> He is gone like the choices
> He is gone like the voices
> He is gone like the hero to sea

As Henry's reputation grew, so too did his songwriting rate, and after three years he was able to quit his construction job. But for Henry, wealth was not what he was looking for in his songs. He wanted simply to share what he felt called to do. What the muse wanted him to do. He wanted to honor the rawness of her, the beautiful surrender when she took hold. And when the muse took hold of Henry, she used him to write love songs.

Henry connected easily with old souls, but the connections were always fleeting. He found the eyes of old souls behind lunch counters, at airport terminals, train stations, and dive bars. His old soul would hook into another old soul and they would both feel a pull. And for a passing moment, they would feel recognized. Then the relationship would vanish back into the past, both of them walking on, feeling full and lonely at the same time.

Henry held a quiet confidence and a disarming ability to observe and feel the people he was with. He was authentically curious about people and, as such, people were drawn to him. They would share their most personal stories and often catch themselves revealing secrets that they had kept covered in shame for years. Henry was a soft place for secrets to land.

With Henry, people knew that their lives were appreciated and their shortcomings unjudged. And in that ease, they would share the messiness of their human experience. Because he listened, people would share. Henry took it all in stride, seeing the tales of miscalculations and poor judgment as evidence that the spinning wild world was nothing more than a beautiful mess of melodies.

Henry typically let his connections with people flow through him, knowing that his musical muse had already taken claim of his heart, but on occasion, he would indulge in heated attraction. Once, he made love to a woman an hour after they met at a songwriters party at a colonial mansion in Nashville. They both felt the pull of old carnal magic. They spoke less than five sentences before they ended up in a guest room together. The woman called out Henry's name so loudly as she reached orgasm that the partygoers in the living room below hushed their conversations, cleared their throats, and caught each other's eye with a sly smile.

Henry could not say where his muse lived. She would share words and melodies in his dreams from some far-off place. And with the vanishing nature of dreams, if he did not write the songs down just after waking, they were gone. Even when the songs were sold, he was prone to forget them. He would hear a song on the radio and not recognize it as his own until a friend pointed it out.

"Holy shit, Henry, that's your song!"

"Really?" Henry would say.

Once his songs were handed off, they were simply things from the past that no longer held him.

By the time Henry was in his mid-thirties, he was flying between Nashville and LA, meeting with producers and artists alike. He sold thirty songs when he was thirty-five and made enough money to buy a small condo from a producer in the Hillview community in West Hollywood. Henry was content renting a small apartment a few blocks from the beach, but a producer in a dry spell offered Henry his condo for a steal. Henry was not one to turn down a deal, and in LA, deals were never farther away than a producer whose field had run fallow.

Henry's best investments came from producers who hit hard times. The same producer that would take him out for steak dinner one night would offer him a watch or guitar for quick cash the next. Henry acquired his blue 1978 Land Cruiser FJ40 from a producer looking to settle a debt.

"I can't pay you now, Henry, but I'll give you my ex-wife's car. It's worth more than I owe you, but I want the goddamn thing out of my driveway."

Henry took the bus to the producer's house the next day.

"Good riddance," the producer said as Henry drove away in the old blue Land Cruiser.

Something about the worn leather seats and clackity-clank of the diesel engine made Henry feel at home.

The producer's ex-wife left a cassette of Frank Sinatra's greatest hits in the tape deck. When Henry switched on the radio for the first time, he was greeted by Ol' Blue Eyes crooning about summer wind. As he drove the Land Cruiser along Highway 101, Frank's smooth baritone filled the vehicle. The Pacific Ocean sparkled with the always-blue sky as Henry unrolled the window and patted the dashboard.

"I dub thee 'Frank.'"

It was a fitting name, Henry thought. After all, the Land Cruiser's light-blue paint was the same color as Sinatra's iconic eyes.

Henry sold most of what he owned within a week of the leaving-dream. His house sold in three days. Real estate was hot in LA and the sale of the condo, along with what he received when his parents passed, left Henry with enough money to live easy in the old cabin on Alder Island. Henry put three T-shirts, three button-down flannels, and two pairs of jeans in his old leather duffle, loaded his guitar into Frank, and bid the Hillview condo complex goodbye.

Rose

Rose graduated from Gonzaga with honors and was accepted into the master of fine arts program at the University of California, Berkeley. She focused on her studies and did her best to ignore advances from men who buzzed around her beauty like flies. She only fell for one of them—a poet with dark eyes and an easy smile. She met Jean-Luc during her second year of grad school when she was studying in France. They would drink rosé and smoke cigarettes on the *Parc du Champs de Mars*. Rose would sketch the Eiffel Tower while Jean-Luc wrote poems. He was much older than Rose, and everything he said seemed flavored with wisdom. It was not so much his knowledge or his actual wisdom, she realized later, but her perception of him that she fell in love with. An older man with art in his soul and passion in his eyes.

Some of Jean-Luc's poems were good. Most of them were not. But his voice…Rose still sighed when she thought about his beautiful voice. It made her feel like she was walking over warm sand. When the cigarettes and wine were gone, they would return to his flat overlooking the gardens of the Rodin museum and play vintage vinyl on his record player. They would drink more wine, talk about art, and color, and words, then make love with the windows open. He was the only man that really seemed to "get" her.

Rose went so far as to envision them getting married and living in the French countryside. She was smitten to the point where she did not trust her eyes when she saw him one day on the Champs de Mars with another woman. The woman had dark hair, like hers, but she was shorter with larger breasts. A different flavor. She watched him kiss her, his hands in her hair.

Rose left France brokenhearted and disenchanted with men, especially with those claiming to be poets. But she loved the art, the music, the gardens, and the language. And in retrospect, she concluded that to fall in love in Paris was worth the heartache.

A friend introduced Rose to Simon as she was approaching the end of grad school. Everything about Simon worked on paper, and when she thought through the match, logic beat her questioning soul. His confidence, easy smile, and clear direction in life won her over.

Simon proposed six months after their first date. A traditional proposal at a restaurant near Berkeley. They both played their roles well; Simon on his knee, Rose with her hands over her mouth as if she hadn't seen it coming. When Rose graduated from Berkeley, she put down her paintbrush and put her energy into building a family. Simon took a residency in Spokane, and the world came together.

They renovated a Victorian home near where she grew up. From her bedroom window, she could see the woods where she danced as a child. During the renovation, Rose walked through the house with Simon, flipping through a stack of paint samples. She showed him how a color could change from room to room and how emotion could come from color.

"Doesn't this color of blue make you feel alive?" Rose said. "Look how calming this is in the afternoon light."

"Blue." Simon shook his head. "I just see blue. Pantone number 292C, blue. I don't understand why you have to attach meaning to everything, darling. It's just blue."

When the children aged into elementary school, Rose actualized her dream of owning a gallery. She wanted to spend her days surrounded by art. And although inspiration for her own work had drifted away, she found joy in elevating the work of others.

The gallery came together quickly and became her safe haven. But as she settled into the space, she began to feel as if she were living around her life, not in it. As if she were watching her own life unfold on the walls. Her life felt like someone else's painting.

Henry

Henry took the on-ramp for I-5, Frank's small engine whining as he down-shifted and pressed the accelerator. He adjusted the rearview mirror and reached up for a pre-rolled cigarette that he left between the sun visor and the roof. He was not a smoker, but he always kept a cigarette in the visor for special moments. He figured leaving LA qualified. *That's what life is*, Henry thought, *just a string of moments.*

He rolled down the window, inhaled, and let the smoke roll over his face. He drummed on the steering wheel and settled into the far right lane at fifty-three miles per hour. The hum of Frank's engine at fifty-three created a low rumbling note that Henry used to harmonize with. He would hum scales up and down as Frank rolled on, steady and sure. Henry had written a hundred songs to the sound of Frank at fifty-three. It was Frank's sweet spot and the two of them worked in tandem to craft the music of the road.

As Henry passed the exit for San Fernando, he was lost in a melody. The din of Frank's engine kept him on pitch as he sang:

Grant Gosch   Kingfisher Lane

Headed north of nowhere
with nothing on my mind
A thousand miles to go
only five miles behind
I get to live this life of mine a second time
Where will you take me, yellow line

Rose

Rose sat cross-legged on a stool behind the service counter paging through the latest edition of *Sunset* magazine. Her favorite song played through the speakers in the ceiling. The lighting was perfect. The light was what pleased her most about her gallery–the pendant lights over the counter and the natural light streaming in from the bay windows that overlooked W. Riverside Avenue. It all worked together to create a sense of reverence and calm.

She had hung a series of landscape paintings from an artist in Idaho on the wall across from the service desk that morning and she wanted to do the artist justice with the right light and angles. She walked across the gallery and adjusted the corner of a painting. A little up, a little down, then back to where it had been. She walked back to the stool, sat down, and picked up her magazine. She stood again and edged at the corner of another painting. A cloud dimmed the bay windows. The room darkened, the paintings lost their color, then the cloud passed and revealed the room in full light.

Rose looked at the family photo that she had propped up on the service counter the day she opened the gallery. Alex was on Simon's shoulders, Rose's arm around Simon's waist, the twins, Ada and Anna, arm in arm in front of Rose. She blocked the image of Simon with her thumb. *Vanish,* she thought. Then, *No! I don't want that. Why does my mind do that? Why would I even think that? I love Simon.* The words rang hollow in her mind. She tried them in her mouth. They did not fit there either.

She remembered how alone she felt the night after taking the photo when Simon had made love to her in the rented lake house. Tears slid down her cheeks when he rolled from her and fell asleep. Being intimate with Simon felt to Rose like putting a plug into an unwired socket. Just action. No electricity. *How is it*, she thought, *that my husband can be inside me and I can feel so empty?*

Tears brimmed her lower eyelids as she looked at the image of her family. The twins were so beautiful and so very different despite their shared time in the world. She wanted to reach into the photo and touch them. She wanted to pull them out and show them the paintings on the gallery wall. "Look, babies, look how the light makes the paint come to life."

What would Alex do if he were here? The little mess. Rose had made a point to hang every painting in the gallery four feet off the ground. At that height, Alex's fingertips could only skim the bottom of the frames. Alex explored the world with his hands and Rose was no exception. It was wildly overstimulating but there were moments when Alex and his hands would make her heart swell. When Rose read him bedtime stories he would reach up and feel the contours of her face.

"You feel pretty when you read, Mommy."

Rose would bring him in tight. "I love you, sweet boy."

Another shadow crossed the gallery wall and the front door opened. "Kind of bright in here, isn't it?" Simon said as he strolled past the new installation. He did not look at the light on the wall. "How is it you can keep this gallery looking so clean and tidy but the house is a wreck?"

Rose felt her blood pressure rise. "There are not three children at the gallery, Simon."

"Yes, I know that. I just think this hobby of yours is distracting you from what's important."

"My gallery is not a hobby, Simon. And it is important."

Simon glanced to the side and made a sucking sound between his teeth. "What was it you wanted to talk about?"

"Lunch. I wanted to have lunch with you. That's what I said this morning. Lunch."

"You know I can't do lunch today. I've got a full caseload."

"You nodded when I asked you this morning."

"Well, you must not have had my attention because I never would have said yes to lunch today. Besides, we went out last week."

"We went to a party last week. I saw you in the car on our way there and on our way home."

"I know, but we were together." Simon tilted his head to the side. "What is this music?"

"'Love like Honey.' It's one of my favorite songs. I played it for you last week."

Simon made the sucking sound with his teeth again, then glanced down at his pager. "Shit! I've got to go, Rose. I should be home for dinner. Try to have it ready before six tonight. I'm meeting my golf friends at seven for drinks."

Rose flinched when the door shut behind Simon. She calmed herself by looking at the filtered light hitting the ceiling above the gallery wall. The slow flutter of leaves from the birch tree outside created dancing shadows. She watched the shadows mold together then flutter away. *Away*, she thought. *Away*.

Henry

Henry inherited the cabin on Alder Island when his parents passed. They died weeks apart. His mother first, from breast cancer. Her loss left Henry locked in grief for months. Then, two weeks later, in the home where Henry grew up, his father's heart gave out. His father's death did not rip him like his mother's, but instead felt like the last glug of a draining tub. A final note to signify what had been. The neighbor found his father slumped by the bird feeder. His mother loved birds and after her death, his father would sit by the feeder and look for her spirit in the finches and sparrows as they flicked at millet and sunflower seeds. One day, he saw her in the eyes of a sparrow and followed her home.

Henry sold his childhood home in Seattle but kept the cabin on Alder Island. The little cabin on the Salish Sea had always felt more like home to Henry than the large Victorian Tudor where he grew up. He was surprised by how easy it was to let one thing go and not the other.

He let the cabin sit for years after his parents' deaths. Then, the morning after his leaving-dream, Henry called Arthur Lee, a childhood friend and carpenter on the island, and told him he was coming home.

"Well, we will be glad to have you back, Henry, but that cabin of yours is a shithole now. The forest reclaimed the yard, the footbridge over Oyster Creek is rotting out, and the big wind storm last year ripped the shingles off the north side of the living room. Nature has had her way, Henry, and your cabin did not put up much of a fight. To be honest, it looks like a squatter's shack."

Henry smiled into the phone. "Henry the squatter. I like that."

"Yes, it does suit you," Arthur said.

"I'll need a hand this summer, and lucky for you, I don't know any other carpenter on the island. You're hired."

As Henry drove north, he eased himself back into the memories of his childhood summers on Alder Island. He remembered his father reading the *Wall Street Journal* on the porch as his mother taught Henry about the geology and natural history of the area. His father provided the quiet steady in the family, but it was Henry's mother that taught him how to fish for salmon, how to chop firewood, and how the natural world is connected. It was his mother that taught him to follow his dreams. She would pick up a shell or a sea star, hold it out to Henry, and say, "We are all part of the natural world, Henry. We are all made of the same stuff. But we each have our individual purpose. Listen to what your heart tells you. Listen to your dreams. This little life is too short to not follow your dreams."

Henry and his mother would spend lazy afternoons walking Kingfisher Lane. They would walk up to where Kingfisher Lane met Orchard Road, then turn back and descend to the bottom of the lane. They would pass the trail to their cabin, cross over the bridge that spanned Oyster Creek, then stop at the wall of brambles that separated Kingfisher Lane from the property of a bed-and-breakfast to the south.

He remembered one such walk when his mother saw a floating log near the shore at the end of Kingfisher Lane. Her eyes twinkled as she waded out into the water and balanced herself on the log. She put her hands out to the side and looked at Henry.

"Take risks in your life, Henry!" She yelled as the log bobbed and swayed. A moment later the log rolled and she splashed into the water. She surfaced again, laughing, her hair dripping wet. She pushed her hair from her face, revealing her hallmark smile. The same smile she had passed on to Henry. "It's better to fall in while trying than stand there watching!"

Henry took her challenge and ran down to the beach, waded into the water, and balanced on the log. The log rolled hard to the left and he splashed into the water next to his mother. She hugged him.

"Yes, Henry! Exactly! Sometimes you just have to go for it! Risks be damned!"

The mile-long walks along Kingfisher Lane solidified Henry's friendship with his mother and infused the day with a sense of wonder. At the end of a walk in late August, Henry noticed a cedar sprout pushing through the mud near the footbridge over Oyster Creek. It was trying to grow on a temporary patch of land in the middle of the creek, its purchase sure to be washed away with the September rain. The cedar sprout reached up to the sun while its shallow roots set into the wet ground.

"Cedars like to keep their feet wet," Henry's mother said. "Look for mud and you will find the cedar trees. Unfortunately, I don't think that little tree will make it."

Henry looked at the budding sprout with sympathy, then pulled it up, root and all, and transplanted it in front of the Kingfisher Lane road sign. He figured watching the tree grow through the years would be the perfect form of island entertainment. By its third year of growth, the tree had edged past the eight-foot signpost and obscured the sign from the road. That summer, the Island County Department of Transportation took the sign off its post and nailed it to the cedar tree.

Every night after dinner, Henry and his parents would sit on the porch, look out over Emerald Pass, and listen for the sound the sun made when it disappeared over the horizon. Henry's father said if they were all very quiet they could hear it: a shallow "woosh" when the sun broke past the round of the earth. Once, at the end of the summer when Henry was ten, he heard it. *Woosh*, then orange, then dimming darkness. Henry dreamt that night about the sun and the light it left behind as the earth spun away. He woke with a song on his lips.

> Good night bright sun
> I'll see you tomorrow
> Good night bright sun
> In darkness I feel sorrow
> Good night bright sun
> Come back to me
> Good night bright sun you are free

Henry held a guitar for the first time at the cabin. He was thirteen years old. Henry's father purchased the guitar from the display window at Thelma's thrift store thinking the instrument would help Henry pass the long summer days. His father sat the guitar next to the fireplace and smiled knowingly at Henry's mother as Henry looked up from the book he was reading, stood, and walked straight to the instrument. The guitar felt familiar in his hands like something returned to him. Henry missed playing the piano in their Seattle home and the guitar helped fill the void. He took it with him everywhere he went. He played the guitar as he walked down the beach looking for oysters. He played it as he walked down Kingfisher Lane. The guitar became part of him, an appendage as familiar as his hands.

Rose

Rose turned her attention from the dancing shadows on the ceiling to the magazine on the service counter. She thumbed through the pages, stopping at a photo of a middle-aged couple standing on a rocky beach. They were framed by the Olympic Mountains. A pair of kayaks sat on the beach next to them. The woman leaned her head on the man's shoulder. His rounded pink cheeks rose from a full white beard. His arm was wrapped around the woman's back, his hand on her hip. The title above the photo read: Alder Island Artist Retreat.

Rose ran her thumb over the photo and took inventory of the couple in the magazine. They were jolly-looking with sunburned faces and adorned in a hodgepodge of wool and fleece, both propped up with a pair of matching rubber boots. Rose looked more closely at the man in the photo and smiled when she saw a feather woven into his beard. *He looks like Santa at Burning Man*, she mused. She ran her eyes down the page and scanned the article.

"Island House owners Gale and Bob (Feather Beard) welcome you to a four-day artist retreat on scenic Alder Island.

Enjoy guided beach walks, home-cooked meals, and beach dance sessions inspired by the movement of the Salish Sea."

Rose looked at Bob again and cringed at the thought of the large man undulating in time with the waves.

"Bring your sketchbook, your imagination, and your appetite. Leave your worries, fancy clothes, and children at home. Call now to book your summer session."

Without thinking, Rose picked up the phone and dialed the number. The phone rang five times and then went to voicemail.

"Helllooo, you have reached the Island House! If we don't pick up the phone right now, we are most likely out on the beach or…."

Rose heard the lifting of a receiver, then dual greetings from opposing voices.

Woman's voice: "Hello."

Man's voice: "Hello."

Woman's voice: "This is the Island House!"

Man's voice: "Island House!"

Woman's voice: "I've got it, you old coot! Hang up."

Man's voice: "You hang up!"

"No! Damn it, Bob, you've been in the garden, I bet your hands are filthy, and I know you didn't take off your boots when you came in." The phone went quiet. "Did you take your boots off, Bob?"

Quiet again.

"My boots don't come off during the day, unless you give me a good reason to take them off." The man laughed into the receiver. "They go on in the morning and off at night! I can't reach down that far more than twice a day."

"GET OFF THE PHONE, BOB!"

Click.

"I'm sorry, my partner is not house-trained. Now, where was I?" The woman cleared her throat. "This is the Island House, how can I help you?"

Rose smiled into the receiver. "Hi, I'm interested in your artist's retreat."

"Oh, fantastic! We are booked up most of the summer, but we have an opening the third week of September. I'll go ahead and put your name down. You don't need to bring much–just a sketchbook if you have one and wine. Don't forget wine. What is your name, darling?"

Rose hesitated. She had meant the call to be informational, not transactional. "Rose. My name is Rose."

"Rose! What a beautiful name. All right, I've got you booked for the third week in September. I'm putting you in the cabin next to the main house. I can tell from your voice you need this retreat, so don't back out. What is your address? I'll have Bob put the information packet in the mail this afternoon. These errands are the only thing that get him out of my hair."

Rose shared her address.

"Okay, I've got it, darling." The phone went quiet. Then, a muted voice behind a hand covering the receiver. "Damn it, Bob, there are boot prints all the way through the front room! I just swept this!"

Gail's voice returned. "Okay, darling Rose, we have you down for the third week in September. It's a quiet week but the most beautiful of the year, in my opinion. Now, I've got to go wrangle a crazy old man. See you soon!"

Click.

Rose pulled the receiver from her ear and looked at it, uncertain of what had just transpired. She set the phone down, then flipped open her calendar. She found the last week of September, and wrote, "Rose Alder Island trip." She looked at the word "trip" and felt a spark of adventure in her chest for the first time in ten years.

Henry

It was well past sunset when Henry made Sacramento. He stayed at a roadside motel called the Pine Cone Inn. He preferred the well-used, one-level motel over the more modern Super 8 for the eclectic staff and storied guests. The following day, he and Frank headed north on I-5, coffee splashing, music playing.

It was 750 miles from Sacramento to the ferry dock in Seattle. Henry figured he could make the journey in fourteen hours. Maybe a quick stop in Eugene to stretch his legs along the Willamette River. Maybe not. Henry had learned that when it came to dreams, one must move quickly and stay on course.

Henry made Seattle before midnight and rolled Frank onto the 11:50 p.m. sailing to Alder Island. The gibbous moon was high in the sky as the boat revved its massive diesel engines and pushed away from the dock. Henry walked to the front passenger deck of the ferry and sat on a wooden bench, breathing in the briny sea air. Thirty minutes later, the dark form of the island came into view. The lights of the ferry dock sparkled green and red as the boat approached the north end of the island. Henry returned to Frank and sat on the hood as he watched the dock workers wrap ropes around large cleats. *Home*, he thought.

Henry drove Frank off the ferry ramp and up the hill toward town. He was at the head of a long line of cars and he watched in the rearview mirror as one by one the cars turned off onto gravel drives and dirt roads. Frank was the only car on the road by the time he arrived at the blinking red light that marked the center of town. Downtown looked the same as he remembered. A couple of stores had changed names, but the gas station, movie theater, and the one blinking stop light remained untouched by time. Such little change was refreshing after living in LA, where house after house was knocked down to make room for something new, modern, and temporary.

Henry turned right at the light and then left onto Orchard Road. He motored south along Emerald Pass, watching the flash of moon reflect off the water through gaps in the trees. As Henry made his way to the cabin, his heart settled into place. He had a nostalgic awareness of each turn as if dancing with an old lover. So familiar, but unexplored by the new iteration of self. A new life in an old place. Moments later, Frank's headlights crossed over the sign for Kingfisher Lane. A line of rusted nails ran thirty feet up the cedar tree he had planted as a child.

Henry guided the Land Cruiser down the lane until he came to the gravel drive that led to the cabin. He pulled into the overgrown hollow in the trees, taking note of the wheel tracks in the mud. *Arthur must have been here earlier today*, Henry thought. He drove past the old maintenance shed, the roof covered in moss, the exterior in need of paint, and parked outside the leaning carport. He pushed open the door, letting the wet air roll over him, then he reached into the back seat and gripped the leather handles of his duffel. He felt around in the bag for his headlamp. The moon hung low in the sky, leaving the path from the carport to the cabin shrouded in darkness, and despite being able to navigate the trail in pitch darkness as a boy, he did not want to chance his safety to childhood savvy.

Henry stepped onto soft dirt and stretched his arms above his head. He took a deep breath, listened to the familiar babble of Oyster Creek, exhaled, then flipped on the headlamp and walked down the trail to the cabin. He paused at each switchback to rest his hand on a familiar tree and sniff at the scent of home. The path was smaller. The trees larger. Each switchback marked by a change in scent. First earthy and wet, then brackish, then salty. He paused in the middle of the footbridge over Oyster Creek. The sound of the rushing water recalled the recent rain. He turned off his headlamp and listened to the flow of the creek, the breaking waves, the slow drip of wet things.

The cedar stairs sagged under his weight as he stepped onto the front porch. *Jesus*, Henry thought, adding "stairs" to his mental list of things that needed attention. He crouched down and reached under the lip of the top step, running his fingers along the wet wood until he found the key hanging from a framing nail. Henry pushed the rusted teeth into the lock and twisted. After some protest, the lock clicked and the Dutch door swung open. He reached inside the door and flipped on the light. Nothing. Henry added lightbulbs to the list as well. He flipped his headlamp back on and scanned the inside of the cabin. It was clear that Arthur had done a once-over on the place but, despite the attention, the house looked of neglect and smelled of mildew. Henry walked across the living room to the west-facing windows and swung them open. Then he returned to the front door, unlatched the top portion of it, and swung it wide to get a cross breeze.

He brushed his teeth at the kitchen sink, then pulled a lightweight sleeping bag from his duffle. He unrolled the sleeping bag on the living room couch, took off his boots and lay down. He was worn-out and road-weary but sleep refused him, leaving him to toss about in his sleeping bag like a climber before a summit attempt. He was well into his mental list of cabin repairs when the sound of the creek and the wind in the trees finally lulled him to sleep.

***

Henry and Arthur spent the next two months working through a long list of repairs and adjustments to the cabin.

Henry wanted to make the place feel like home before winter set in, and the morning chill spoke of an early fall. They took out the wall between the two small bedrooms at the back of the house to create one large bedroom that spanned the width of the cabin. Henry put a new queen bed next to the French-paned window on the south end of the room. He liked to leave the windows open at night so he could listen to the whisper of Oyster Creek.

By late July, Henry and Arthur had replaced the cedar shingles on the north side of the cabin, repaired the rotten wood on the porch stairs, and reinforced the bridge over Oyster Creek. There were a few adjustments to make on the chimney flashing, but Henry had a larger priority.

The final effort of the season was to bump out the northwest side of the living room to accommodate an upright piano. Henry found a used Steinway at an estate sale in Tacoma and enlisted the services of the only moving company on the island to have it delivered. It was a tight fit, but the bump-out on the north side of the living room, along with new floor supports, worked to accommodate the instrument.

When the piano arrived, the movers refused to take it down the treacherous footpath to the cabin so it was up to Henry and Arthur to manage the task. Arthur constructed a dolly with fat rubber wheels made just for the purpose of transporting the six-hundred-pound instrument down the trail. They worked together like a curling team, with one man clearing the path of debris, the other guiding the piano over rocks and around the switchbacks. On the third switchback, an off-camber rooted section, Henry slipped and the Steinway leaned heavily to one side, threatening to tumble over Henry and down into Oyster Creek. At the last minute, Arthur hauled heavy on the dolly strap and fought the instrument back onto the trail. Henry looked up from where he slipped and wiped his brow.

After pushing the piano across the footbridge, they put rounded creek stones under the dolly wheels and sat down on the porch to catch their breaths. Arthur took off his gloves and leaned back on the piano.

"Why don't we just leave it here?" he said with a smirk.

Henry walked to the piano and began playing. The notes rose up through the valley and out over the tidal flats. "I certainly prefer playing outside but the rain would turn her into mush by October."

Arthur sighed heavily, "I guess you're right, for once." Then he stood, brushed off his pants, and looked out over the creek. "You've got a little slice of heaven here, Henry."

Henry smiled. "It's all right."

Arthur walked up the trail to his van, retrieved two steel ramps, placed them in a wheelbarrow, and wheeled them back to the cabin. He nailed one end firmly to the porch and rested the other end on the ground. With three heaves, Arthur and

Henry pushed the piano onto the porch. They rested again and looked up the trail to the parallel wheel gouges that ran through the mud.

Arthur rubbed the stubble on his chin with a calloused hand. "You know, at least with an elephant…it would've walked down here."

Henry smiled. "That's true, but a piano won't take a twenty-pound shit in my house."

Arthur patted Henry on the shoulder. "I'm not so sure about that, I've heard you play."

Henry shoved Arthur in the shoulder. Arthur punched Henry in the arm. It was this way with them.

Henry woke early the following morning and walked stiff-legged into the living room. At forty-two years old, his body remembered the previous day's work before his mind could recollect the assault. He kept himself well-maintained and trim, but he was not immune to the slow creep of age. Henry pulled a chair from the kitchen table and placed it in front of the piano. He sat, sipped his coffee, and tapped at the keys with his left hand. He ran his fingers up the keyboard, searching for out-of-tune notes, then reached above the piano and opened the windows. The sound of wake waves and the low hum of a distant tugboat flowed in with the breeze. The air was rich with the smell of drying kelp and blackberries.

He looked up as he played and spied the fat gull that had taken up residency near the cabin. The gull was in search of a clam that had not been sucked dry by a sea star or moon snail. The gull cocked its head to the side and looked up at Henry through the window disapprovingly. Henry had named him Spectacle because his discerning inspection of shells reminded him of a rotund, pompous jeweler inspecting diamonds.

After observing the bird for two months, Henry realized that Spectacle held avian dominion over the cove. Anytime another bird landed on the beach, Spectacle would spread his wings and waddle over to the visitor, squawking until the weary intruder flew off.

One evening while Henry was reading in the living room, a clamshell fell down the chimney and rolled out of the firebox and onto the floor. He looked out the window and saw Spectacle float down onto the porch railing. The bird began marching back and forth squawking. Henry opened the window and tossed the clam out onto the picnic table. A moment later, the clam hit the roof again, this time from a much higher altitude. Despite the interruption and disapproving side-eye, Henry and Spectacle had learned to live together. Roommates of the cove. And, as the season turned cool, Henry felt very much at home in the world of music, tides, and flying clams.

Rose
(Friday)

Rose had not been alone, alone-alone, in ten years. The children and the gallery took up most of her time. Then there was Simon, who seemed to know her more by expectation than reality, one of those expectations being that she was available at a moment's notice to attend his work events or host a dinner at the house. Simon was a loving husband by all accounts, and in many ways, Rose felt proud to be matched with him; they had worked well together in crafting their life.

But now that the children were becoming more independent, Simon's practice built, and the gallery opened, Rose felt a lonesome ache. Being with Simon felt like being with a teammate after a winning season and realizing you have very little in common other than the game itself.

He was one of the best-known orthopedic surgeons in Spokane. Rose felt proud of him and for her part in his success. He gave Rose space when she needed it and was undoubtedly a good provider. Simon's intellectual view of the world had attracted her when friends introduced them, but she had learned over time that his clinical acumen and intelligence came with an inaccessibility to emotional nuance. He dealt with Rose's feelings when they were hurt as simply in need of repair. Something to be rooted out, examined, cleaned off, and put back in place with a smile. When Rose felt depressed, Simon would send her articles about how she could improve her mood. There was no space to let emotions roll through. She felt like one of his hobbies–providing meaning, pleasure, and annoyance in the way his golf game might.

Whenever Rose's emotions shifted to the whimsical or romantic, Simon would not follow. Instead, he would view her as broken, illogical, or childish. Her whimsy just needed to be fixed up with the appropriate procedure, article, or reminder of how well they had it. Rose tried hard to forgive Simon for not understanding her. He was not mean-hearted. He was just not capable of connecting with her deep and wild places.

"Sometimes I see the pink of the sunrise play on the river and I want to cry. I just feel the beauty of it so deeply. I want to feel deeply, Simon. I want to feel deeply with you."

Simon would respond with a worried expression.

"It's just a color, Rose." Simon would say. "It's light cutting through the atmosphere to create a color, it's nothing to get emotional about."

Rose's heart would break at her soul's response. *Be with me in a way you can't. Know me in a way you can't. Appreciate me in a way you can't.*

Simon's trying was as enduring as it was heartbreaking. But loving him for trying was the love she wanted, and she felt selfish and unfair for wanting more. *It is not Simon's fault*, Rose thought. *Trying should be enough. Endearing should be enough.*

***

Rose spent two days cleaning out the family Volvo in preparation for the trip to Alder Island. Despite the effort, she could not get rid of the animal sticker residue on the rear windows or the ketchup stains in the back seat. She had wanted to take Simon's car, a black BMW convertible, and she went so far as to picture herself driving west on I-90 with the top down, her long black hair swirling around her face as she played her favorite music full blast. When she pitched the idea to Simon, he pursed his lips, exhaled through his teeth, and explained how it was more logical for her to take the Volvo. The Volvo had better gas mileage, the Volvo was safer, and the Volvo could be scratched with less concern.

"Now that the kids are out of car seats, I can fit them all in the back of the BMW, no problem," Simon said. Rose acquiesced. Simon's logical mind was hard to argue with and she did not have the energy to defend her case. The important thing was she was on her own, headed west on an adventure for the first time in a decade.

In the third week of September, Rose backed her Volvo down the driveway and headed for the I-90 West on-ramp. It was a bluebird day; the air was crisp and inviting. Simon had agreed to a weekend alone with the kids and without golf. Rose coordinated with her friends to watch the kids before and after school when Simon was at work. It was a sound plan that led to a wild sense of freedom as she drove through the wheat fields of eastern Washington. She felt like a true adventurer. A past self revisited.

An hour after leaving Spokane, Rose pulled off at the Ritzville exit for gas and coffee. When she came to a stop at the gas station, a Cheerio rolled out from under the passenger seat. She could not escape the evidence that she was, in fact, a thirty-eight-year-old mother of three.

She looked down at the Cheerio and felt a lonely itch for her children, then brushed it aside. *This is my time. It's okay to have my time*, she thought. Nonetheless, as she rolled out of town, she felt a burning desire to point out a roadside sculpture of a farmer and his wife to a backseat audience of future adventurers.

Just after crossing the Columbia River, Rose took the exit for Vantage Riverside Park and coasted down the off-ramp to a parking spot by the water's edge. She had come to the same park twenty years earlier with her high school boyfriend, Charlie. They were on their way home from a concert at the Gorge

Amphitheater when Charlie said, "Let's get naked and go swimming!"

Rose's lips had curled into an always-ready smile.

"Hell, yes!"

Charlie parked his truck in the shade of a willow tree. They stripped down to nothing and ran into the water holding hands. She remembered Charlie holding her from below as she rested weightless on her back, her breasts revealing themselves through wind waves for the world to see. Cars honked from the bridge over the Columbia as travelers looked down at her lean, naked body. She extended both hands out of the water and gave the cars on the bridge the bird, then slipped into the river laughing as Charlie dove in after her. They walked back to the truck and made love in the front seat. She remembered how she looked in the rearview mirror. Flushed and dripping wet.

Rose parked in the same spot that she and Charlie had parked twenty years earlier. The willow was much larger and its hanging branches ran along the roof of her car. It was mid-morning and there was no one at the park as she stripped off her cutoffs and T-shirt. She slipped on her sandals and ran to the river in her bra and underwear. When she dove in, the water and memories washed over her. She floated on her back and looked up at the clear blue sky. No cars honked, no strong arms held her from below, but she floated happily with the remainder of her more buoyant self. A hand raised within her soul. *There you are*, Rose thought. *There you are.* And, feeling the freedom of being alone in the wild of the river, she took a deep breath and dove deep into the cool blue water.

The rest of the journey along I-90 was a leaping of landscapes. The wide open fields of eastern Washington changed to mountain vistas and then deep, green boreal forests. As she descended the west side of the Cascades, Rose thought about the leaps in her own life. Leaps of faith that led to travel, her MFA, and the gallery. She was proud of her choices but wished she had been braver and more thoughtful about some leaps. She thought about Simon and clenched her jaw. In retrospect she saw how a leap to security could land you on a pedestal of loneliness. *But the children*, she thought, *the beautiful children. I would do it again.* She sighed, shook her head, and focused her eyes on the road. *Life and landscape,* Rose thought. *Both change as you move forward. Just keep driving.*

After seven hours on the road , Rose drifted down the final slopes of the Central Cascades and into the tangle of Seattle traffic. Rose held the directions to Island House in one hand as she navigated in a half panic to the Seattle ferry docks. She pulled up behind a VW bus littered with bumper stickers. One read, "That was Zen, This is Tao." Another read, "Be Wild, Child." *Be wild,* Rose thought. *Yes. Be wild.*

When it was time to board the ferry, Rose followed hand signals from a portly man in a yellow rain slicker. She had never been on a ferryboat before and the experience quickly transitioned from quaint to terrifying as she threaded her Volvo through the tight parking deck. When the man in the slicker directed her to turn off her engine, she was positioned at the front of the boat with a clear view of the gray water and darkening sky. The same VW bus that was in front of her in the ferry line was now pulled up beside her. Rose looked over and smiled at the driver, a vaguely familiar man resembling a large gnome. He smiled back a large free-hearted smile, his eyes nearly disappearing into wrinkles. A feather swayed in his Spanish moss beard.

Rose settled in for the ride as the ferry pulled away from the dock. *Not a bad view*, Rose thought, as she looked out over the water and onto the Olympic Mountains bathed in afternoon light. She reached into the center console and padded around for a snack. All she could find was a pack of goldfish crackers and a fruit cup. She opened the fruit cup and tipped it to her mouth, tapping on the bottom to release a stuck maraschino cherry. She washed it all down with a sip of cold coffee from her travel mug. She was about to refill her coffee from her thermos when she remembered the wine in the cooler.

The registration packet from the Island House included a packing list. Wine was mentioned three times. Rose took the suggestion to heart and filled an Igloo cooler with her favorite wines. She reached into the back seat, popped open the cooler lid, and fished out a bottle of rosé with a screw top. She looked both ways as if someone might reprimand her, then with a flick of the wrist, unscrewed the lid and poured the wine into her coffee mug. The man in the van next to her looked over and gave her another wide smile, this time with a thumbs-up. Rose raised the mug and toasted him through the window.

After finishing her wine, she ventured out onto the ferry. Rose had a hard time sitting still when adventure was at hand and exploring the ferry boat was no exception. She always wanted to see what was around the next bend and was known to bring her car to a screeching halt to read a roadside marker or take in a new view. Rose's intense curiosity was of particular annoyance to Simon. Once, on the way to a soccer game, Rose did a full U-turn in afternoon traffic to look at a rainbow.

"Adventure!" she'd yelled as she put the car into a g-force turn.

Simon had eyed her with annoyance. "What the hell, Rose! Stay on track!"

Rose was greeted by the smell of saltwater and the tang of diesel fumes when she opened her car door. The vibration from the boat's engines ran through her sandals and up the inside of her legs as she walked to the back of the car to retrieve her sketchbook from her backpack. Rose followed the signs for the passenger deck and pushed through the heavy metal door to the stairs that led to the ferry's main sitting area. She paused at the base of the stairs when she realized she had left her camera in the car. She thought to turn around, but decided at that moment to document her journey only through sketches in her journal.

Rose scaled the stairs to the passenger deck and turned toward the bow of the boat. She passed rows of green vinyl benches that ran along the perimeter of the ferry and smiled at families eating clam chowder and playing board games. She dismissed the soft note of guilt for not being with her own children, then leaned into the freedom of being on her own. She pushed through the doors that led to the outside passenger deck and felt the chill of September wash over her. She was wearing denim cutoffs that she had crafted from a pair of vintage jeans and a gray hoodie. She looked down at a dark stain on the sweatshirt and thought back to when Alex used it to clean a full packet of mustard off his face. Rose shook her head at the realization that her clothing had become a memoryscape of food mishaps.

Rose watched the island approach from the passenger deck while her hair blew over her face and the whir of the ferry engines echoed along the water. "Be wild, child," she whispered into the wind.

Rose returned to her car just as a rush of whitewater boiled up from the front of the boat as it reversed its engines and eased into the dock on the north side of Alder Island. She set her sketchbook on the passenger seat and left it open to a rough outline of the ferry. She reviewed the directions to the Island House, running her finger along the route from the ferry dock. The directions were printed on a photocopied image of the island, and when she looked more closely, she saw that the island was more like two islands pinched together into an isthmus at the north and south ends, like two quarter moons stuck together at their points. She was thinking about how she would sketch the island from an overhead view when the portly man in the yellow slicker returned, tapped lightly on the hood of her car, and mouthed, "GO." She started her engine, released the emergency break, and drove onto the island.

Taillights stretched up the hill in front of her as she wound up the steep tree-lined road from the ferry dock. When the hill leveled off, Rose felt like she had driven into another country. The landscape reminded her of Scotland, and the houses were less modern than what she had seen in Seattle. She glanced down at the directions as she passed an old yellow barn with a bear-paw-quilt pattern painted below the north-facing gable. Feeling pressure from the cars behind her, Rose pulled off to the shoulder and let the procession of cars, trucks, and motorcycles roll by. She got two quick beeps from the man in the VW van. He flashed her the peace sign as he passed.

Rose read the directions twice more as a means of settling her travel-weary mind. It had been a long day and she did not want to miss any turns.

Drive up the hill from the ferry terminal
Right at the stoplight in town
Left on Orchard Road
Look for the Island House sign 1/4 mile past Kingfisher Lane

Rose set the directions on the passenger seat as butterflies beat about in her stomach. She took a breath and let the feeling wash over her. It was an old feeling and, although slightly uncomfortable, she welcomed the nostalgia of it. Feeling excitement for something new was something she had not felt in years. *Just north of comfort*, she thought. *My growing place.*

A soft mist fell through the trees and layered up in beads on the windshield as she drove. The day was running itself out and the slant light melted the afternoon into the cool, even dim of evening. Rose turned on her headlights, checked the rear view, and accelerated back onto the highway.

She drove comfortably without the pressure of cars behind her, turned right at the stoplight in town, then left on Orchard Road and headed down a winding, leaf-scattered drive. She passed a sign for Kingfisher Lane and a quarter-mile later found the hand-painted sign for Island House. The tension in her shoulders eased with the realization that the directions had not led her astray.

When she arrived at the bottom of the hill, her eyes swept over a mossy sign marked "Parking." She pulled in next to the same VW bus that she had seen on the ferry and, in that moment, the image of the man in the magazine came to her. His white beard with a feather woven in. *This is already becoming a small island*, she thought as she opened her car door and surveyed the property through the mist.

Henry
(Friday)

Henry and Arthur made a tradition of stopping work early Friday nights to play music on the front porch of the cabin. They looked out over the water and sang old country tunes, their voices reaching deeper into Emerald Pass with each drink. After one rousing run through "Walk the Line," Arthur suggested that Henry play with him on stage at the next farmers market.

Henry leaned back in his chair and shook his head. "Hell no."

Arthur narrowed his eyes. "You've got songs playing on the radio around the world but you're too much of a chicken to play at the farmers market?"

"Yes, yes I am," Henry said.

"Okay, how about this." Arthur stood up, steadied himself, and set his mandolin on the picnic table. "Let's race for it."

Henry laughed. "What the hell are you talking about, Arthur?"

Arthur pointed at the footbridge over Oyster Creek. "If I can beat you in a foot race to the Kingfisher Lane sign, then you will play two songs with me at the farmers market tomorrow."

Henry smiled at the challenge. "Well, shit, Arthur, I don't think you could beat me to the end of the porch with those little legs of yours."

Arthur raised a brow as he leaned down and stretched his hamstrings. Halfway through the stretch, he staggered and caught himself with the porch rail. Seeing a window, Henry leaped up from his lawn chair and ran across the porch and down the front steps toward the footbridge. He shoved Arthur in the shoulder as he ran by.

Henry was halfway to the first switchback when he heard Arthur screaming like a wild man behind him. Henry instinctively looked back, missed a step, and tumbled into a clump of ferns. Arthur hopped over Henry's legs, but not before Henry reached up and grabbed one of Arthur's feet, causing him to belly-flop onto the trail. In an alcohol-inspired feat of gymnastics, Arthur bounced up from his chest and took off up the trail, full throttle.

Henry shook his head, rolled out of the ferns, and stumbled to his feet just as Arthur disappeared around the second switchback. Henry, with his long legs and natural athleticism, reeled Arthur in and they were neck and neck when the trail opened up onto Kingfisher Lane. From there it was a thirty-yard dash up the gravel straightaway to the road sign and Henry knew he had the advantage. He was pulling into the lead, with ten yards to go, when he saw a Volvo station wagon drive past the mouth of Kingfisher Lane. He caught the profile of a dark-haired woman, her hair pulled back behind her ears. He noticed the soft round slope of her forehead and her Scandinavian nose. Henry lost his focus and Arthur slapped him hard on the ass as he accelerated for the win.

Arthur leaned with one hand on the cedar tree at the top of Kingfisher Lane, catching his breath, and looked to Henry with a smile. "The songs I'd like to sing are 'Walk the Line' and that song you wrote a few years back. What's it called? Something about love like honey? I'll sing harmony, you sing the melody."

Henry put his hands on his head, breathing deep as he watched the Volvo's taillights turn down the gravel drive to the Island House. Henry sighed and looked back to Arthur. "Don't pretend like you know how to sing harmony. What you do is more like tossing notes at a song, hoping to get lucky." Arthur grinned at Henry and slowly extended his middle finger as he turned and walked back down Kingfisher Lane, singing in a trill voice.

> Henry and Arthur ran up the hill
> To race for a song
> Henry slowed down when a car rolled round
> Distracted by his dong.

Henry shoved Arthur in the shoulder. "I should have beat you," Henry said.

"You're right!" Arthur said. "You should have."

Later that afternoon, after Arthur headed home, Henry sat at the piano drinking tea in hopes of staving off a hangover. He looked out over the porch and onto Emerald Pass and saw a salmon jump near the mouth of Oyster Creek. The season was changing and the shift was marked by yellowing leaves and leaping fish. Just as Henry settled into a melody, Spectacle flew past the window, squawking. Henry followed the bird with his eyes and saw a dark-haired woman at the south end of his cove.

She was barefoot, sandals in hand, wading through the shallows. Henry brought his shoulders back and straightened himself as he watched the woman move through the water. She was graceful in her stride. *A dancer*, Henry thought. The woman leaned down and picked a rock from the beach. She tested its weight in her hand, then leaned back and tossed the stone in a low arch over the water. Henry watched, motionless. The stone sailed off at a shallow angle and then skipped. When the stone landed, it rolled over the surface tension in quick hops before disappearing into the depths. It was a fine skip and Henry had half a mind to yell out and congratulate the dark-haired woman. Then he thought how odd that would seem: an unknown man sitting at a piano, in a cabin, yelling through the evening to congratulate a stranger on her stone-skipping prowess. Henry shook his head, pulled his gaze from the woman on the beach and returned his hands to the piano keys.

Rose
(Friday)

A cedar-chip path ran from the parking strip up to a two-story home that Rose could only describe as "eclectic" in its design. A concrete bulkhead ran along the water's edge in front of the house. The bulkhead was flanked on either side by massive madrone trees that reached out and touched the water with their smooth maroon limbs. The house was a rustic blend of remodels and its charm came from aggregation rather than design. It looked like a sedimentary project that had incorporated pieces of design ideas and hopeful intentions as it rolled through a long history of owners.

Rose learned from the magazine article that the house was built in 1923. The only original attribute was the fireplace hearth and chimney constructed from the same granite stones that were strewn along the beach. Just to the south of the house sat a small cottage with a sign above the door that read *The Barnacle*.

The cottage wore a set of weathered stairs that led to a covered porch. Its shingle roof was dotted with moss, and a narrow chimney poked out of the rear gable. *Home sweet home,* Rose thought, as she reached into the front seat and fished out her sketch pad. She leaned against the car and drew the rough angles of the house and cottage. Five lines for each. Just enough for form. *Something to be revisited later with color*, she thought.

Rose gathered her backpack and walked stiff-legged to the main house. As she made her way across the gravel drive, a rotund woman in her sixties opened the screen door and waved to Rose as if she were welcoming a daughter home from college. The woman was adorned with a gap-toothed smile, a purple fleece jacket pocked with tiny burn marks, black nylon hiking pants, and calf-high wool socks.

As she waved to Rose, she called out in a camp-counselor tenor, "Hello, Rose Stephenson. Welcome home!" Rose searched for a witty response, but all she came up with was a hesitant wave.

"My name is Gail! We've been waiting for you. Welcome! Welcome! Welcome! You are in *The Barnacle*." She pointed to the cottage next to the house. "The door is open! Put your things away and then come join us for tea, if you'd like."

Suddenly, Gail jumped and let out a wild screech. Rose flinched as she watched Gail wheel around and howl, "Damn you, Bob! You old shit!" The bearded man from the ferry appeared from behind Gail with a mischievous grin. He had delivered a solid spank on Gail's rounded haunch just as she finished her salutation.

"You must be Rose! I'm Feather Beard. I saw you on the ferry! May I call you Wild Rose?" Rose nodded slowly as Gail went about swatting the man with an open palm.

"Not everyone needs a nickname, you big ogre!" The bearded man ducked down and jumped to the side with agility misaligned for someone of his proportions.

Gail turned back to Rose. "I'm sorry. That wild beast of a man is Bob. He calls himself Feather Beard for obvious reasons. He's got the memory of a squirrel so he gives everyone he likes a nickname. He blew into my life ten years ago like one of those filthy feathers he keeps in his beard and now I can't get rid of him."

Rose gave Bob a two-fingered wave. Bob curtsied. "Welcome to the Island House, Miss Wild Rose!"

Rose turned and walked back over the gravel drive to her station wagon. She opened the rear hatch and pulled out her backpack and hiking boots. Then, using her head, she nudged the rear door down and slammed it shut with her knee, a move she'd perfected through countless trips to the grocery store with children in tow.

Rose shouldered her pack, appreciating the familiarity of its weight. The old Jansport had logged countless miles on her back after college and it wore a patch from each country she'd visited. Rose and her backpack had traveled together over the cobbled streets of Rome, the Scottish highlands, and the beaches of southern Thailand. *Together again,* Rose mused. *Same pack, older woman, softer bed. I hope.*

Rose swung open the door to the cottage and ran a hand along the inside wall in search of the light switch. She found the switch at the back of a shelf, a sure sign of a remodel. She flipped on the light and surveyed the room. A small fireplace with a stone hearth sat on the south end of the room. A kitchenette with a two-burner electric stove and small oven was nestled into the corner on the southeast side of the cottage. Near the window, overlooking the water, was a door that opened into the bedroom.

She spent ten minutes making the cottage her own by adjusting the light. Rose loved the feelings that came when light was perfectly aligned to her mood. A flickering candle, a fire in winter, a sunset in fall. She noticed how her mood could change with the angle of the sun as it ran along the sky. Light was paramount to any experience and she wanted her time at the cabin to be perfect. And like anything perfect, it started with light. Rose walked through the cottage adjusting the shades until she felt at ease. Then she opened the door to the bedroom, sat her pack on the floor, closed the curtains and melted into the goose-down comforter.

Rose woke an hour later to the sound of a distant foghorn. She stretched, then looked around the room. She checked her cell phone and felt a rush of anxiety when she realized there was no reception at the cottage. She scanned the room for a landline, finding nothing but seashells and coastal art on the shelves. She sat with the nervous feeling of being out of touch, then quickly talked herself down. Simon would be fine with the kids; her friends could help if he were called into the office. *Let go of what you can't control.*

Rose unpacked her backpack and organized her belongings. She made a scrupulous effort to keep this trip to the essentials. *Only what I can fit in my backpack,* she'd thought as she packed. No extra jackets, no out-on-the-town outfits. The only thing she had packed that did not have some form of child-inflicted stain was a forest-green dress she bought at her favorite boutique in Spokane the day before the trip. It called to her from a rack and she instantly pictured herself wearing the dress while sitting on the porch of Island House, reading a book and sipping wine. Rose lined up her boots, sneakers, and sandals next to each other by the front door.

Light and symmetry, she thought. *Give me light and symmetry and I'm a happy woman.*

Rose slipped on her sandals and walked from the cottage to the beach. The sun was fading into purple and she stopped at the water's edge, listening to the soft melody of the waves unfolding themselves on the rocky shore. She turned northwest, chasing the light and the setting sun and scanned the beach for skipping stones as she walked.

After a quarter mile, the shoreline rounded into a cove. The bend in the landscape kept the cove hidden and sparked Rose's always-curious mind. She slipped off her sandals and waded around a downed tree that blocked her path. When she rounded the corner, she looked up to see a small cabin tucked into the trees next to a creek. The cabin had a layer of fresh shingles on the north side of the porch giving it a patchwork appearance that was accentuated by the setting sun. As Rose walked farther into the cove, she heard music floating down from the cabin. She saw a man through the cabin window leaning over a piano, his shoulders rocking slowly with the notes he played. Quick notes followed by longer, deep chords. A voice swept over the water. A baritone. Soft and low. A welcoming voice.

Rose found herself wanting to sketch the moment. She wanted to capture the beauty of the place and the way the evening light played off the man's hair as it hung loose over his face. She thought to yell out and tell him not to move, to stay just like that until she could retrieve her sketch pad and watercolors. *How ridiculous that would be*, she thought. Rose laughed at herself and looked down into the shallow water. Her eyes caught on a dark oval stone. She reached down, picked up the stone, and tested its weight. When she drew back her arm, the music stopped, the night quieted, and the sound of the skipping stone ran uninterrupted along the water.

Henry
(Saturday)

Henry woke early the morning after seeing the dark-haired woman in his cove. A dream clung to his consciousness like mist in the trees. He rolled over, reached to the nightstand, and trailed his fingers along its surface until he found his journal. He put pen to paper and wrote what he could remember of his dream.

The dark-haired woman was standing in his doorway. It was early morning, before twilight. He could see the angles of her body but not the details. She walked to him, placed a soft kiss on his forehead, and slid into bed. He turned and looked in her eyes, startled by their familiarity. They were beautiful and green, like pools of jade. The dark-haired woman looked through the piled-up grit of his life. She ran a hand over his cheek, down his neck to his chest, and placed her fingers over his heart. Henry's body heated north and south from where her hand rested. Then she slid a long graceful leg over his body and settled herself on top of him, her heart beating in time with his.

Henry attempted to write the words to describe the scene but he could only find themes. Darkness. Heat. Warmth. Depth. He closed the journal and squeezed his eyes shut, hoping to return to the dark-haired woman, but the dream was gone. He breathed deep the morning air, then kicked the covers from his legs and walked to the window on the north side of his room. Purple light teased the top of the Olympic Mountains, and the Salish Sea rolled slow and calm. Henry watched a seal pup and its mother break the surface of the water. He edged the window open and put his elbows on the sill, then leaned out over the side yard and listened. The morning was so quiet. Nothing but the sound of the seals breathing as they bobbed in the slack tide.

Henry left the window open, retrieved his journal, and walked to the piano. He sat down, rested his fingers on the keys, and placed a bare foot on the cool brass damper pedal. It was the first time a melody found him before the words. Usually, the words appeared from the muse like a poem. Without melody.

This was different. This was just emotion. Something unto himself.

Henry tapped middle C and D over and over, then he circled around the notes with other keys looking for a connection. "Where do you want to go?" he asked, speaking softly to the notes. A moment later he found another dream note. He played the first and second note back and forth. Each stroke of the key brought an image from his dream. Henry opened himself to the music and waited for the muse to arrive with her words. She never came.

The sun had shifted halfway down the Olympic Mountains when Henry stood from the piano and walked out onto the porch. His cove was secluded from the north and south as it curved inland toward Oyster Creek, creating a U-shaped estuary that was inaccessible from the beach at high tide. It was a private place and other than the dark-haired woman, Henry had not seen anyone on the beach in the three months since he'd arrived. He liked it that way. The privacy of the place. He enjoyed the quiet and the way the wind swirled around his body as he stood on the porch with nothing between him and the world but the sea and his dreams.

After a breakfast of farm eggs and garden greens, Henry pulled on his favorite blue flannel shirt, put his guitar in its case, and walked up the footpath to the carport. He strapped his guitar case into Frank's passenger seat and tightened the lap belt. The drive from Kingfisher Lane to town was marked by hard turns and Henry had learned the hard way to always secure his guitar after it had bounced out of the seat and knocked him in the temple.

He turned Frank left on Orchard Road and drove north at a lazy cruise. The speed limits on the island were generally thought of as a rough estimate and most islanders puttered along at whatever speed felt right. The general feeling on the island was a laidback twenty miles per hour unless there was a ferry to catch. In that case, the serene country roads would turn into a speedway of rusted-out vehicles and luxury cars, all trying to best their time to the ferry dock, dropping hubcaps as they rounded corners.

Henry spotted Arthur's Datsun at the back end of the farmers market parking lot. The car was easy to pick out with its corrugated plastic rear window and multicolored side paneling. The passenger door handle had been replaced with a bottle opener.

"It's a piece of art," Arthur would say.

"It's a piece of shit," Henry would respond.

Henry pulled in next to Arthur's rolling art installation, unbuckled his guitar, and made his way through the parking lot to the market. He patted the roof of Arthur's car for good luck as he walked by. It was just before noon and the farmers market had yet to get underway. Old trucks lined the perimeter of the open-air pavilion as islanders in overalls moved produce and crafts into their assigned booths.

Just to the south of the pavilion was a large lawn where families would spread blankets and picnic on sundry food purchased from the market. At the end of the green was a covered stage. Henry spotted Arthur on stage, tuning his mandolin. Arthur looked up, strummed an out-of-key chord, and motioned for Henry to join him.

"Looks like a good crowd today," Arthur said, as Henry walked onto the stage. "I'd say it's one of my best!" Arthur nodded to the four people milling about on the green.

The Arthur Lee Show had been a standing act at the farmers market for three years running. The island newspaper described Arthur's "show" as a wrestling match between his kazoo, mandolin, and vocals, all working against each other to create something like music from 12:30 p.m. to 1:00 p.m. The organizers of the event had given Arthur the earliest and shortest time slot as a means of limiting his musical assault on islanders and tourists. Arthur sang exclusively original work that no one knew or seemed to want to know. The songs he wrote featured love affairs between sea creatures and aliens, and each song would include a variety of voices and characters acted out with wild enthusiasm.

Henry opened his guitar case and looked at Arthur. "All right, you sly son of a bitch. Two songs, then I'm out of here."

Henry tuned his guitar as Arthur leaned over and whispered, "Whatever you say, slowpoke."

Arthur strummed the first chords of "Walk the Line." Henry followed along and soon they were both lost in the music and unaware of the people assembling around the stage.

When the song was over, Henry looked up and was disheartened to see that a significant crowd had gathered. They all clapped as Arthur stretched his arms out and bowed like a carnival host. Henry stepped back from the mic and gave the crowd a nod as Arthur addressed the audience with exaggerated arm movements.

"I want you all to welcome back to the island the only man I know with three first names, Henry David James!"

The crowd clapped and Henry swore under his breath. Despite Henry's obvious discomfort, Authur continued, "This sorry bastard headed off to LA when he was eighteen, only to realize the real magic of this world is right here on the island."

The audience cheered louder.

"Now, he's written a number of songs that you all may know, but none of them are very good. Especially this next one." Arthur nodded to Henry and began playing the intro to one of Henry's most well-known songs. Henry edged up to the mic while glaring at Arthur. Then he closed his eyes and blocked out the growing crowd.

I saw her in the moonlight
Dancing like the rain
Summer all around her
Moving like a flame

> I held onto her body
> Like honey holds the spoon
> I lost my heart in Texas
> Under a full moon

Henry opened his eyes to the sound of cheering as people recognized his song. As he looked out over the crowd of unfamiliar faces, he caught a glimpse of shoulder-length black hair. He watched as the woman from the beach traversed the lawn toward the pavilion. She looked up and caught Henry's eye. Henry stopped singing. She smiled at him and Henry lost track of the music altogether. Arthur took the lull in Henry's singing as an invitation for a solo and began blowing his kazoo like it was on fire, small beads of sweat forming on his forehead. Henry returned to himself, finding the words as the dark-haired woman disappeared into the crowd.

The Market
(Saturday)

Rose walked slowly through the rows of vendors in the pavilion, appreciating the variety of arts and crafts the island had to offer. The man on stage had to be the same man she had seen singing in the cabin the night before. She was sure of it. He had the same sweet voice and long hair. He was singing her favorite song in a way that made her soul vibrate. She stopped mid-stride and felt something move in her heart. She looked up to the stage and took a breath. The stage was much closer than the cabin had been and she was able to make out his features. His tanned skin rounded along the bones of his face, his flannel shirt snug across his chest. She could see the contours of muscle under the worn fabric. But it was his eyes, his dark eyes, that stopped her. The intensity of them caught her off guard. His eyes held hers and looked into her, speaking words to something hidden away. She figured he must have been looking past her and into the crowd at someone he knew. And if not–if he was looking at her with that intensity–Rose's heart beat faster. *Well, that would not be good. The last thing I need to do is make eyes with the locals,* Rose thought.

The crowd erupted in cheers as Henry strummed the last chord of his song. An older woman in the middle of the audience yelled, "Welcome home, heartbreaker!" Henry tucked his guitar back into its case and elbowed Arthur in the ribs as he walked off stage. When he made it to the bottom of the steps, he was greeted by a small group of adoring fans who claimed to have known him. He hated this part of performance–the obligation to know others or hurt their feelings. He returned their hellos, then ducked through the crowd as quickly as he could while handing out his standard "Thank you" and "Good to see you too."

Arthur's voice rolled in from behind, "Ladies and gentleman, sweet little Henry David James, all grown up!" The crowd cheered. Henry casually waved, then gave Arthur a scowl as he walked past a group of people sitting on a picnic blanket, eyeing him. A few more slaps on the back and Henry was able to disappear into the ambling buzz of the market.

When he made it to the safety of the pavilion, he stashed his guitar next to the exit, then reached into his pocket and pulled out an unorganized handful of bills. He counted the cash, smoothed them into a small fold, and put them back into his pocket. Fifty-three dollars. *Enough to get me through the week,* Henry thought as he walked to his favorite farm booth. The farm was run by the Medics, a husband-wife duo in their mid-forties. They both had long blond hair, and if it weren't for Carl's broad shoulders, it would be impossible to tell them apart from behind.

As Henry approached the booth, he saw the Medic children behind an assortment of vegetables. The youngest of them, a girl, held a bunny in her lap while the two boys played a game of catch with a dirty head of cabbage. Carl put his boys in matching headlocks as he greeted Henry.

"Good to see you, music man! What time can I drop these three mistakes off at your cabin?"

Henry laughed. "Well, if they like fixing leaky roofs and yelling at Arthur, they can come by anytime."

Henry opened the cooler that sat on the table between a basket of eggs and a bowl of blackberries. "What do you have today?"

Carl smiled. "Goat cheese, goat milk and…." He reached into the cooler and grabbed a chop of meat. "Goat! We still have some Levie left. He was a good goat but he ate Kim's roses, so… now he's on sale."

Henry smiled at Kim, who had looked up from arranging goat cheese wedges on a tray of ice.

"Remind me not to eat your roses."

Henry selected a small portion of goat cheese, then picked out a dozen eggs from the bowl on the table. He looked down to a stack of children's finger paintings that were for sale. One of the paintings was of a barn that looked to be floating on water; another was of stick-figure goats that appeared to be mating; a third, from the youngest, was just green finger strokes.

"What's this one?" Henry asked the girl as she gently stroked the bunny in her lap.

"A green blanket," the girl responded without looking up.

"I'll take it!" Henry put the eggs, cheese, meat, and painting into a bag, counted out thirty dollars, and handed it to Carl. "Keep the change."

Carl reached under the table and grabbed a bottle from a hidden cooler. He handed it to Henry with a wink. "Take this too. Made it myself. It's multipurpose; you can drink the cider and then you can hit Arthur with the bottle."

Henry took the bottle and lifted it toward the sky. The brown liquid shot rays of amber onto his face.

"It's hard cider from the August apples," Carl said. "It's a bit bitter, but so is life."

Henry tucked the bottle under his arm and nodded to Carl. "I'll put it to good use."

Henry turned and walked along the rows of booths until he came to a table full of flowers. His eyes held on a bundle of lavender. Henry had always loved lavender. His dad would buy a bundle for his mother every time they visited the island, and his mother would work the lavender into a bouquet along with ferns from the trail to the cabin. Henry picked up the lavender and smiled at the woman behind the table.

"Do you want me to make you a bouquet with that?" she asked.

"Sure," Henry said, "as long as it's less than twenty bucks. That's all I have left."

"I can work with that," the woman said with a wink. She took a handful of wildflowers, daisies, and fern stems and laid them on the table with the lavender. She bunched them together and tied them with a hemp string. She handed them back to Henry and smiled. "Nice job singing. Welcome home."

Henry looked down at the flowers, feeling bashful. "Thanks."

He took the lavender bouquet, retrieved his guitar, and headed back to Frank. As he rounded the last booth in the pavilion, he came face to face with the dark-haired woman. She looked at him, smiled, then looked down at the flowers in his hand.

"Those are beautiful," she said.

Henry stood motionless, lost in her eyes. The same green eyes he had seen in his dream. "Yeah."

The dark-haired woman cocked her head with a puzzled expression, then moved to the side to let Henry pass. He found himself searching for words. He wanted to tell her that he saw her from the stage, that he saw her on the beach, that he saw her drive past Kingfisher Lane, that she appeared in his dream. But all he was able to do was wet his lips and adjust his weight from one boot to the other. Rose smiled as she felt his eyes looking into her. Then she looked away, feeling startled by the tightening in her chest. Henry's eyes settled on the curve of her lower lip. It caught him off guard–the sweep and angle of it.

The woman spoke again.

"I hope you have a wonderful day. And I love the song you sang. It's one of my favorites." She looked to the stage and then back to Henry. "Henry, is it? I think that's what your friend said."

Henry nodded. "Yes. Henry."

"Well, Henry, I'm Rose. It's a pleasure to meet you."

Henry wanted to shake her hand but his arms were full and all he was able to do was stick out a pinky. Rose looked down at his pinky and took it between her thumb and pointer finger. She shook it like she was turning on and off a light switch.

"Hope to see you again, Henry." Rose sidestepped, smiled again, then walked past him and into the crowd.

Henry
(Saturday)

Henry took the long way home, looping Frank around the south end of the island before heading north again and back to the cabin. The backroads always put his mind at ease, each turn feeling like a meditation. When he came to a long stretch of gravel, he slowed Frank and reached into the back seat for the bottle of hard cider. He pulled the cork out with his teeth, took two sips off the top, tasted the sour of the apples, and set the bottle between his legs. He reached down and ran his thumb over the lip of the bottle as he thought about the shape of Rose's eyes. Perfect crescents at the crown of her nose. Her eyes swept up slightly, coming together in faint lines that appeared in more detail when she smiled. Her cheekbones framed the delicate sweep to her jaw, leaving her with an expression of warmth and wisdom. There was a small scar on her forehead. *A story. I want to know that story*, Henry thought. Then he found himself tracing the angle and form of her lips on the cool curve of the bottle neck. Swoop and curve. Her features seemed like an already known thing. *How beautiful and tragic to feel such things for a passing soul*, he thought. Henry took another sip of the cider and sang along to the hum of Frank's engine.

> Headed home
> With you on my mind
> Water all around me
> Looking for a sign
> I don't know you
> But I know this heart of mine
> Falling for you sweet sublime

He was deep into the song when he passed by the island thrift store and caught the silhouette of a fly-fishing rod through the large display window. Henry squeezed the bottle tight between his legs and swung Frank into a sharp U-turn. He downshifted and rolled the Land Cruiser slow and easy into the gravel parking lot. He walked to the display window and looked at the fly rod through his own reflection. It was an old bamboo rod. A classic. Just what he had been looking for. Henry walked into the store and surveyed the hodgepodge of bric-a-brac that lined every available inch of real estate. A gray-haired woman with a mischievous grin looked up at him from behind the service counter.

"Mmm, mmm, mmmm, look at you, handsome! You have kind eyes."

Henry gave her an awkward smile. It was an unusual greeting and he did not know the proper way to receive it.

"When I see a new person in the store, I like to say the first thing that comes to my mind. Sometimes, I should bite my tongue, but I figure, what the hell! I'm an old lady, I can call 'em like I see 'em, and you…you, friend, are handsome and have kind eyes. Now, welcome to Thelma's Thrift Shop. Believe it or not, I'm Thelma!"

Henry motioned to the fly rod in the window. "How much for the fly rod?"

The woman tapped her cane on the floor with a loud pop. "I knew that's what you wanted! Gol, darn, I told myself someone is going to come into this store today and buy that fly rod and that someone is going to be a beautiful man and that someone is going to make old Thelma's day and you are that someone and darn-it-all, my day is made!"

Thelma tapped her cane twice more, then hobbled out from behind the counter. She was hunched but surprisingly quick, her cane seeming more a stage prop than needed support. Henry followed her to the window as she flipped her cane upside down and used the hook end to grab the fly rod just below the reel. She pulled it out of the mannequin's hand and swung the rod between an easel and golf bag in one seamless motion.

"The fly rod is thirty bucks, the cane is not for sale, and the old woman is free if you want to take her home!" Thelma laughed and knocked her cane again on the floor.

Henry shifted his feet.

"Don't worry, darlin', old Thelma is harmless, mostly." She winked at Henry. "Now, that rod comes with a whole mess of tackle, or flies, or whatever it's called. I'll fetch it for you and you can buy that from me too."

Henry followed as Thelma shuffled to the back of the store and pulled a dusty shoebox off a shelf, handing it to him. He opened the box and peered down into a tangle of rod parts and hand-tied flies. Thelma tapped the box with the crook of the cane.

"You know what? I'll throw these in for free if you promise to come back and let me look at you."

Two more taps of the cane and Thelma turned and headed to the service counter.

Henry looked at the "cash only" sign on the register, reached into his pocket, and came up with nothing but guitar pics.

"Damn it, I just remembered, I spent the last of my cash at the farmers market," Henry said.

"Well, now! This is my lucky day," Thelma said with a slow roll of her shoulders. "Now, you take that fishing rod and that mess of tackle in the box and you just come on back whenever you get the money. That will give old Thelma something to look forward to. Hot damn, a two in one."

"Are you sure about that? I can go to the bank."

"Heavens, no! Just stop in with the money next time you're driving by so I get to see those brown eyes again."

Henry nodded. "Well, that's awfully kind. Thank you, Thelma. "

Henry turned to go.

"Wait!" Thelma yelled. "What's your name, stranger?"

"Henry James. I just moved into the cabin on Kingfisher Lane."

"Well, that's one of the most beautiful spots on the island! Some say it's sacred ground." Thelma eyed Henry over her glasses. "Wait just a moment. James, you say?"

"That's right," Henry said.

Thelma smiled wide. "I sold your dad a guitar years ago! Hot damn! What a small world. Now, don't make me wait too long to see you again!"

"Yes, ma'am." Henry nodded.

Thelma motioned to the door with her cane. "Now, if that door is locked when you stop by, you can walk around back to my apartment and hopefully you'll find me in bed." Thelma cackled and thumped her cane again as Henry turned and walked through the door.

Lost in Light
(Saturday)

Henry walked down the trail to his cabin with his guitar in one hand and the fly rod, groceries, and flowers in the other. He set the rod on the porch and used his knee to turn the knob on the front door. He put his guitar on the couch, left the groceries, painting, and flowers on the kitchen table, and walked to the piano with the bottle of cider. He opened the windows on either side of the piano and let the cross breeze blow over his face. The melody from his dream came to him and he tested it with words.

> I saw you there
> Moonlight in your hair
> Right in front of me
> By the rolling sea

Henry sang the lines over and over as the afternoon light pressed into evening. He was excavating with a light brush. Not pushing the song. Letting it come to him as his voice drifted out the windows and over the beach. As Henry jotted down the chord progression, he saw Spectacle rise up past the window, squawking his high-pitched staccato cry. The cry that meant an intruder, avian or otherwise, had wandered into the cove. Henry looked out the window and scanned the top of the fir trees for an eagle or osprey. Finding nothing in the trees, he looked down to the beach and ran his eyes along the cobbled shore until they came to rest on Rose, looking up at the cabin.

Henry's fingers went numb. His heart caught on something deep and sticky and he felt himself cleave open. He took a breath, then stood from the piano bench and gripped the neck of the hard cider, looking for the cool curve of the bottle neck to calm him. He walked out through the front door and onto the porch. He tried to focus on the texture of the wood under his feet, each grain, each sunken nailhead, anything to pull his attention into the moment.

He put a hand up and waved as he approached the porch rail. Rose's sandals were in one hand and a piece of sea glass in the other. She raised her hand with the sea glass and it caught the light. A blue spark. A small thing. A beautiful thing. Henry tilted his head at the indigo flash. Rose looked over her shoulder at the water. Red, orange, and purple reflected off the small wind waves. The Olympic Mountains were dressed in strokes of pink.

"It's like a painting," Rose said, her voice raised just enough for Henry to hear.

"You should see it from up here."

Rose turned back and looked at Henry. The setting sun and the light from the cabin made him appear as if he were in a pop-up book, a two-dimensional person in front of a two-dimensional cabin.

Rose yelled back, "Okay."

Henry hadn't meant the words to be an invitation and Rose had not meant to accept. The words just found each other.

Henry thumbed the deck rail as he watched Rose slip on her sandals and pick a path around the large rocks that dotted the beach. When she neared the berm that separated the beach from Henry's property, she paused and looked up at him.

"There's a path just to the south," Henry said, pointing to a thin foot trail over the berm. Rose followed Henry's direction with her eyes and spotted a thread of trail running through the seagrass.

Rose suddenly became conscious of herself. Her movements, how her clothes held her body, the way her cutoffs slipped up and down her thighs as she walked. She had intended to go for a quick stroll before cooking herself dinner in her little cottage. She brought her sketch pad. She wanted to sit on a piece of driftwood and draw the cabin, so there was no reason to wear anything but her dirty denim cutoffs and fleece jacket. But now, as she walked through Henry's front yard, she felt exposed and vulnerable.

Rose stood halfway across the yard looking up at the cabin as Henry approached. The setting sun bathed his face in pink light. There was a kindness in his eyes that seemed to appraise her and disarm her at the same time.

"Hi, Rose."

"Hi, Henry."

Henry searched for words. "Do you like cider?" Henry asked. "Carl gave me a bottle at the farmers market today and it would probably be best if I didn't finish it off myself."

Henry held the bottle out to Rose and realized his intro was not quite right. She had no idea who Carl was and he probably looked like an alcoholic hermit standing there with a wine bottle in his hand.

Rose gave Henry a smile. "Well, I'd certainly hate to disappoint Carl."

They walked together across the flagstone path that led to the cabin stairs. Just before they reached the stairs, Rose stopped and leaned down to pick a rock out of her sandal. Her hair fell forward and framed her face. When she looked up again, the sounds of the world quieted for Henry. Like closing a door. Like turning the radio all the way down.

Henry noticed the way her hand rested on the railing of the stairs. There was something so familiar about her long, graceful fingers. The skin on her hands was smooth like the bark of a madrone. His heart sank when his eyes came to rest on her wedding ring. Rose saw a shadow cross his face, then disappear again, as his eyes swept to hers.

The sunset, having turned deep orange, brought Henry back into the moment and the flow of the creek became audible again. And again, he could see the ferns, the cedar trees, the light hugging Rose's angles from behind.

As Rose scaled the last step, she looked past Henry to the view over his shoulder. She felt his eyes on her, but they did not feel hungry or threatening. Instead, she felt as if she were simply being admired. Rose took a deep breath and held it for a moment. Henry was right–the view was stunning.

When she exhaled, Henry was by her side. He extended his hand out to her. "I was hoping to try this again."

Rose laughed and took his hand. His fingers were long and graceful. Warm and inviting. She felt a row of calluses where the fingers met the palm.

"My name is Henry James. Good to meet you."

Rose looked up from his hand and smiled. "Rose," she said. "Good to meet you… again."

A bashful glance from Henry. "Come, have a seat."

Rose's eyes held on the contours of Henry's back as he walked across the porch. His flannel rested snug across his back and she could see the outline of his strong shoulders. Shoulder, shoulder, shoulder. Rose moved the word around in her mouth. She liked the way it felt to say, the way her tongue touched the roof of her mouth when she said it. Shoulder.

"Have a seat," Henry said again, looking back at her while motioning to a pair of folding chairs that looked out over the water. "I'm sorry it's a bit rustic. I'm still in the folding chair stage of settling in."

Rose sat and Henry handed her the bottle of hard cider.

"Let me grab some glasses. Feel free to sip out of the bottle in the meantime," Henry said as he turned and walked to the front door of the cabin. He smiled with his eyes, thankful his humor hadn't melted into the warm space between himself and Rose.

Henry walked into the cabin and found himself looking over the scene as Rose might. The hammer on the wood stove, yesterday's beer bottle on the window sill, folding chairs, mason jars, one bowl in the sink. The only redeeming feature was the bouquet of lavender that sat on the counter next to the stove. Henry one-handed two mason jars from the cupboard next to the sink and picked up the lavender as he walked back to the porch. He set the mason jars and the bouquet on the table.

Rose appreciated the contrast between the quiet, bearded stranger who wrote love songs and the warm-handed gentleman who awkwardly set flowers on the table. *What is it about contrast that is so attractive,* she thought. A strong man with a light touch. Reserved power. Hard things and soft things weaving into threads of balance.

Rose tipped the bottle of hard cider over the jars and filled them halfway. Pouring the cider gave her a measure of control in this new place with this new person. She set the bottle on the table next to the bouquet as she took in the view. The sunset, the water, the beach, the flowers and cider. She thought about light. How the last fifteen minutes of the day were the most dynamic. How light creates shadows and shades of color shifting into something darker and quieter. She took a breath and looked at Henry and they passed a silent conversation.

I'm married. I have three children.
I want you to know that.
Henry looked out over the water.
I write songs.
They come to me in my dreams.
Last night I dreamt of you.

They let the silence sit between them.

"So, this is your every night?" Rose tipped her jar toward the setting sun.

Henry nodded slowly. "Yes. I mean, sitting with a woman is a first. Usually, it's just me. Or me and Arthur, if it's Friday afternoon."

"And Arthur is…?"

"I'm sorry. Arthur is a carpenter of sorts, a friend of sorts, a musician of sorts. He lives just up the beach. He is the only person I've spent much time with since I've been back."

"So, that was Arthur with you on stage today?"

"Yes, exactly. I lost a bet."

Rose raised her eyebrows. "Why did you lose?"

"I got distracted." A quiet moment held between them.

Rose broke the silence and took the lead in the conversation. "When he was on stage, Arthur said you used to live here. What brought you back?"

Henry leaned back in his chair and looked out over the water. "A dream."

"A dream?" Rose repeated.

"I lived in LA for many years and I never saw anything as beautiful as this." Henry nodded out toward the water. "I dreamed it. A few months ago. I dreamed about coming home. So I just followed the dream."

Rose smiled at the words. "Do you always follow your dreams?"

Henry sat back in his chair and chewed on his bottom lip. "So far. Yes."

Rose smiled at Henry, disarming him with her bright eyes. "A dream follower. That's a good thing to be."

"It hurts a little sometimes, but I think that's a good thing. To hurt a bit for your dreams."

Rose let the words sit in. "The song you sang, 'Love like Honey,' you sang it from your heart."

Henry wiped his brow with his hand. He did not like claiming the songs he wrote but a part of him wanted Rose to know. "Well, that's kind of where it came from."

"What do you mean?"

"I wrote it."

Rose looked at him through the quiet night. "You wrote it!"

Henry smiled.

"Oh my god, Henry. I… you…"

Rose felt temporarily starstruck, then found her bearings.

"You are a talented man. That is one of my favorite songs!"

"It's just the words. The artists bring it to life."

Rose settled herself and after a few starts and stops, the conversation flowed into music and art. Rose shared a story about walking the streets of Paris with a canvas, taking note of how the color showed up differently during the course of a day and how it made her feel different things. Henry talked about words and how they sometimes flowed together like water over ice, and how sometimes they got stuck inside him like a button too big for its hole.

Their words melted into the evening as the western sky emptied itself of light. The houses along the beach on the other side of Emerald Pass sparkled as the rhythmic wash of the waves became louder and closer to the house.

"Can I interest you in another drink?" Henry asked.

"I should go," Rose said. "I'll lose the beach if the tide keeps coming up."

Henry nodded into the darkness. "I'm afraid the beach is already gone. There is an old trail to the bed-and-breakfast at the end of Kingfisher Lane. That's where you came from, yes?"

"Yes."

"I'll show you the way."

"I guess one more drink would be okay, then." Rose lifted her glass to the rising tide.

Henry took the glasses and walked back to the kitchen. He found an unopened bottle of bourbon on the shelf above the stove, rinsed the glasses, dropped in ice, and walked back to the porch. When he returned, Rose was standing at the porch rail running her thumb along her thigh.

She turned to look at him. "I should go."

Henry set the glasses down on a porch railing. "Yes. Yes. I understand."

Henry retrieved the flashlight that hung on a hook just inside the front door. He switched it on and a dim cone of light nudged at the darkness. He frowned.

"You need batteries," Rose said.

"Yes. True. I'll add it to the list. I know the way. I'll save the light for the slippery parts."

Henry led Rose down the front steps and across the yard to the footbridge. When they were halfway over the bridge, Henry stopped. Rose bumped into his back and instinctively put a hand on his shoulder.

He turned.

"Listen," he said, putting his finger to his lips. Rose's heart raced with unknown expectation as she looked at Henry's silhouette through the darkness.

"Listen," Henry said again. Rose quieted her breathing. She heard the rush of water from below the footbridge, then the hush of wind through the alder leaves overhead. Then, she heard something out of tune with the evening. Splashes from the water below.

"They're back," Henry said.

"Who?"

"The salmon. They come back every fall to the creek where they were born. I think they follow some unique mineral in the water that calls them home, although some say they follow the stars. One way or another, they come right back home. There is a spot about a mile up the creek above a small waterfall where they lay their eggs. They pool up below the falls 'til the rain brings the water level high enough for them to finish their journey."

"I'd like to see that," Rose whispered.

"I can show you," Henry said.

"Okay."

They stood silently and listened to the sound of the rushing water. Henry tipped his head toward the splashing salmon and sang quietly.

Welcome home
Welcome home
You've come so far
Welcome home
Welcome home
Guided by a star
And when you leave this place
Your life will be embraced
Welcome home
Welcome home
Welcome home

The night quieted again. Rose smiled into the dark. Surprisingly, Henry did not feel embarrassed.

"Did you write that?" Rose asked.

"Yes, when I was a kid. I used to come up here and sing to them. I thought maybe they could use a little music while they waited for the rain."

Henry leaned out over the rail of the footbridge and felt unexpected childhood nostalgia well up. He hummed the tune, then trailed off. He looked down into the darkness of the creek.

On impulse, Rose reached to him through the darkness, wanting to comfort him. She put a hand on his forearm.

Henry looked down at her hand.

"It's funny–that's the first time I've sung that song in over thirty years."

Rose leaned toward Henry, then thought to pull away, not wanting her familiarity to seem cavalier. But it felt natural in that moment and he received her with a smile. When the moment passed, Henry turned up the trail, body tingling, savoring her touch, and led Rose up the switchbacks to Kingfisher Lane. When they came to the section of angled, off-camber roots, where he almost lost the piano, Henry flicked on the flashlight and guided the way, holding the dim light at an angle that allowed Rose to see the trail. Once they made it to the road, he turned the light off again. Filtered moonlight cut through the canopy, creating moving shadows as they walked side by side down the lane. The crunch of gravel underfoot seemed out of place in the quiet night.

When Henry spoke again it was in a soft tone. "I'm glad to know you."

Rose's heart thudded against her ribcage. This was not expected, this sliding into someone. This untimely dissolution.

Henry turned the flashlight on again when they reached a wall of brambles at the end of the lane. "Looks like the blackberries reclaimed the trail. I guess that happens after thirty years."

Henry searched around under the base of a maple tree until he found a four-foot limb that had fallen in the last storm. He cleaned the limb of smaller branches until it was stripped bare, its green bark wet in the dim light.

"This should do the trick," he said. "Could you hold this for me?" Henry handed the flashlight to Rose as he shaped a trail through the brambles using the maple limb and an overhand swing. Sweat slicked Henry's forehead as a path opened through the woods. A bead of blood appeared on his forearm.

"Looks like a thorn got you."

Henry looked down at his arm and sucked at the blood. "Oh, that just means I'm doing it right. These blackberries only grant safe passage with a sacrifice!"

Henry continued clearing the path as Rose followed behind with the light. A few minutes later, the brambles opened up at a split-rail fence that marked the property line of the Island House.

Henry scaled the fence with an easy stride, then reached out and took Rose's hand and helped her over. They stood together in the field that outlined the property and looked down to the bed-and-breakfast. Moonlight spread out in a glittering arch along the wet grass.

"Beautiful night. Are you in the big house?" Henry asked.

Rose pointed to her cottage. "That's me, The Barnacle."

"It's lovely," Henry said. "I'll walk you there."

Rose hesitated, thinking of Gail and Feather Beard watching from the house. She shook the feeling as best she could, but found herself walking with a light foot and an eye toward the front porch. They walked side by side, leaving a line of footsteps in the grass. As they approached the gravel drive, a motion light on the front porch flicked on.

"Shit!" Rose whispered. A moment later, the screen door creaked open and Gail stuck her head out.

"Rose? Is that you?"

"Yeah! It's me."

Gail opened the screen a bit wider and looked into the night. She saw Henry and nodded slowly. "Okay. Well…glad you're back. I was just about to ask Bob to go looking for you. We saw you walking up the beach a few hours ago and wanted to make sure you didn't get lost or something."

Guilt crept through Rose. She thought about Simon. It was late and he had most likely fallen asleep in the twins' room. She felt a need to explain it all away. *This is nothing. It's just a walk, it's nothing,* she thought.

Gail continued. "Breakfast is at 8 a.m. tomorrow. Just let us know if you will have a guest and we will…"

Just then, Bob appeared behind Gail and put his arm around her shoulder as he sized up the situation.

"Wild Rose, indeed! I know how to call 'em." Gail nudged him in the ribs as he continued. "Glad you found yourself a buddy, Wild Rose! Just let us know if you need extra towels or…" Bob trailed off. "Toothbrush."

Gail stomped on Bob's foot so hard that he cursed into the night, letting the screen door slap shut as they retreated into the house. A moment later the motion light flipped off.

"Are those your parents?" Henry asked.

Rose laughed. "Yes, I think so, actually. At least for the next four days."

"Four days," Henry repeated. "So, Wednesday? You leave Wednesday?"

A quiet moment held in the air between them.

Rose looked to the house as they walked to her cottage and saw the curtains edge open in an upstairs window. She could imagine Bob and Gail looking out at the cottage, waiting for some form of salacious entertainment.

"Yes, I head home on Wednesday."

They stood together quietly next to Rose's cottage.

"I had a wonderful evening," was all Henry could think to say.

Rose smiled. "Tell Carl I said thank you for the cider."

Henry handed Rose the stick he used to knock back the brambles.

"Take this. It's good for clearing out cobwebs along the trail we made if you want to come visit."

Henry handed Rose the maple limb and as she reached out to take hold of it, their fingers touched. Like flint to iron, Rose felt a spark jump its way up her hand and warm her chest.

"Thank you," Rose said.

"I'll show you the falls tomorrow?"

"Yes! I'd like that."

"Okay, I'll come by and pick you up here at high tide, around noon. That's when the salmon head up the creek."

"Okay."

Silence again.

"Good night, Rose."

Henry felt the gravity of her pulling at him, as if she herself held some unique mineral that was calling him home.

"Good night, Henry."

He turned and walked back across the wet grass, taking a wide berth from the house so as not to trigger the motion light. Rose watched him from the cottage. When he arrived at the path in the brambles, the flashlight flicked on. Moments later, the bobbing light disappeared into the tangle of damp forest. Rose stepped inside her cottage and closed the door. She sat down on top of the bed, drew her legs to her chest, and rested her chin on her knees. She felt an anxious excitement, shrouded in guilt, creep through her body.

"Fuck!" she whispered into the night as she leaned back on her pillow and closed her eyes.

ROSE
(SUNDAY)

Rose woke early the next morning to gray light streaming through rain-streaked windows. She watched the light chart a path up her legs. She slowed her breathing and tried to catch its movement. Impossible, it seemed, like watching the rise of the tide. After years of distracted mornings, she reveled in the simple pleasure of the rising sun.

When the light reached her thighs, her thoughts turned to Henry. The warmth of him when she touched him on the bridge. The spark from his hand when they said good night. She thought about his hands. Strong and warm. She thought about the words his hands had written, the keys they had played, and the strings they had thumbed. She thought about his hands holding her. His fingers moving up her neck and wrapping in her hair.

Her body warmed at the thought of his touch. *Just a harmless fantasy*, she mused, as she slid a hand under the duvet and found herself. She pictured Henry's shoulders. Rounded. Strong. The movement of him. Then his hands again. She thought of his fingers brushing her cheek. His hand on her thigh, her hips, her breasts. She rolled to her stomach, the duvet slipping and exposing her legs to the rising sun. Her fingers moved in a slow rhythm. Henry's hands holding her. Her body warming. Henry's weight on her. Her hands on his chest. The heat of him. Her pulse quickened as her mind slid Henry just inside her, then moments later, quietly, fully into her depths. Circle. Slide. Circle. She arched her back as intense pleasure flowed through her body.

Rose relaxed into the bed and breathed in the morning chill. Everything seemed so distant. Her life. Her real life. Perhaps it was being on an island, or the feeling that she was in some way returning to herself. Tears welled in her eyes as raw emotions surfaced through the confusion of her life. Waves rolled along the shore. Small waves. Wind waves. They were close. So close that Rose could hear the tumble of rocks and she felt as if she were one of them. A rock tumbling along to some greater force.

Rose's thoughts were interrupted by the staccato clang of the triangle on the front porch. She looked at the clock on the nightstand; 8 a.m. She rolled from bed and slipped on her shorts, sandals, and fleece. She stretched her arms to the ceiling, exposing her midriff to the cool of the morning. She thought about crawling back into bed but the idea of someone else cooking for her was almost as pleasurable as her orgasm.

Rose walked across the gravel drive and up to the porch of the main house. She was anxious to see how Gail and Bob would react to her after seeing her in the motion light the night before. When she walked into the house, she was greeted by a couple in their sixties–new guests that had arrived the previous evening. They looked up at her from the dining room table.

"Good morning!" they said in unison.

"Good morning!" Rose replied. Not a glance from Gail nor an eyebrow raise from Bob. They were immersed in an argument about the best type of firewood, with Bob arguing that maple burned steady and sure, and Gail arguing that fir provided the best crackle.

When Bob looked up and saw Rose, he smiled. "Wild Rose! You've got to try one of those fresh croissants." Bob nodded to the serving table.

Rose looked at the table and her mouth watered. It was adorned with baskets of croissants, some with almond filling, some with chocolate; fruit and two crystal pitchers of fresh-squeezed orange juice. A bottle of champagne sat at the end of the procession.

Rose filled her plate and sat down across from the new guests. As she began to eat, Gail stood and addressed the group.

"Good morning, everyone! Now that you are all settled, I'll share our schedule with you. Breakfast, as you can see, is at 8 a.m. every day, followed by a beach walk with Feather Beard.

I'll be teaching a watercolor class from ten-thirty to noon. Feather Beard put the crab pots out last night and we invite you all to join us for dinner on the patio tonight, unless he ends up empty-handed… again." Gail winked at Bob who took the insult with a good-natured grin. "All of this is optional, my friends. This is your time and this is your house. If you want to sit on the porch and paint, go for it! If you want to run off and meet a new friend,"–Rose felt a glance from Gail–"by all means, go and do it. Here on the island, we enjoy what life has to offer. We only get a handful of trips around the sun, after all. We might as well enjoy the ride." Gail raised her glass to drive home the point. "Enjoy the ride!"

The guests raised their glasses in return. "Enjoy the ride!"

After breakfast, Rose made her way back to the cottage feeling very much as if she were at adult camp. The sneaking through the woods, the champagne with breakfast. Her own little cottage. Camp counselors. Nicknames. A crush on a man in a different cabin.

After adjusting the shutters in the cottage, Rose stripped off her shorts and fleece. She folded them neatly, placed them on the bed, then walked naked to the bathroom and turned on the shower. The chill of the cottage raised goosebumps along her limbs as she looked at herself in the bathroom mirror. Her impression of herself tended to reflect her mood, and as she stood there looking through the steam, she liked what she saw.

The round of her breasts sat heavier than in her youth. The faint line of tiger stripes along her abdomen that had appeared when she was pregnant with the twins. But in the comfortable set of her breasts, and the stretch of her body, she saw the beauty of having fed life into the world. She looked at the round of her hips and thought about the power of womanhood.

Rose's eye caught on the faint C-section scar just above her pubic bone. She ran a finger along its raised edge and thought of Alex. She remembered how sad she had been when, after hours of pushing, the doctor told her they would need to perform a C-section. The first of many sacrifices that motherhood would demand. Alex was a challenge in birth and in life, and she loved him deeply because of it. Both the scar and the boy were a reflection of how strong she was.

Rose took her time in the shower, relishing in the quiet of it. No one called her. No one interrupted. When she turned the shower off, she walked across the cottage and looked out over Emerald Pass. The coolness from the window tightened her skin. She dressed in her flannel and slipped into a pair of jeans. She pulled on wool hiking socks and laced up her boots, stomping on the floor to test the fit. The sound of her steps echoed through the cottage. It had been years since she felt the weight of hiking boots on her feet and she loved the feeling of adventure they held.

Rose arrived early for the beach walk and decided to bide her time by exploring the library near the fireplace in the living room. As she passed through the front door, she noticed the steep angle of the threshold, the hinges tested by the settling house. She walked past the dining room and into the nook of bookshelves by the west-facing windows. As she passed the kitchen, she heard Gail and Feather Beard talking over the sound of clanging pots.

"The moment I saw that Wild Rose drinking wine on the ferry, I knew she needed a little excitement in her life."

Rose hated eavesdropping but could not help but pause at Bob's mention of her name.

"Well, it seems she's found it. And I tell you, I don't blame her. I've thought about wandering down to that cabin to see if the rumors were true myself," Gail said.

Feather Beard laughed and snapped his dish towel at Gail's behind.

"All I'm saying is that that man is nice to look at. In fact, I think you should invite him down here for dinner tonight. He already seems to enjoy one of our guests and it's about time we get to know our neighbor."

Feather Beard chuckled. "Well, I know Rose wouldn't mind."

Rose blushed outside the kitchen door.

Feather Beard laughed again. "Good thing I'm so good to look at!"

Gail cackled as Bob pulled her into his arms and squeezed her behind. "Get back to work, ogre!"

Feather Beard grunted and returned to washing dishes.

Rose's face felt hot as she walked to the library. She felt exposed in her attraction to Henry.

Let it go. Let it all go.

Rose glanced at her watch. She had twenty minutes before the beach walk and figured she could find an art book to distract her thoughts. She looked through the shelves with a wandering mind, the titles slipping by like things in the distance. Finally, her eyes landed on a book of French sculpture and she blindly flipped through the pages. When she came to a photo of *The Kiss* by Rodin, her eyes held the fingers of the sculpture, then she followed the arm up and around the nameless woman. She remembered being in Paris and seeing firsthand the beauty of the marble. The way the afternoon sun lit the sculpture evenly. It was the right time of day to see Rodin's work. The organic movement of light brought the marble to life.

"Let's walk!" Feather Beard said at drill-sergeant volume.

Startled, Rose jumped and looked up from her book. She couldn't help but appreciate Bob's outfit. He wore a tie-dyed T-shirt with a faded image of Jerry Garcia on the front, an unzipped blue hooded sweatshirt with the sleeves cut off, loose-fitting sweat shorts cut three inches too high, calf-high wool socks, and sandals. The outfit was as eclectic as the Island House and it suited him perfectly.

The other two guests were gathered on the front porch sipping coffee when Rose and Bob arrived. Bob adopted a professorial tone as he shared the natural history of the area, the gull feather fluttering in his beard as he talked.

"Seventeen thousand years ago glaciers carved out the Puget Sound," Bob said, waving his arms in the air to represent moving ice. "The deep fjords that were left behind created one of the most beautiful places on earth. Keep an eye out for large, out-of-place granite rocks as we walk down the beach. Those are Canadian boulders that the glacier shat out as it retreated. But, like most Canadians, they are friendly and good to have around."

Bob performed a little skip step then pointed in the air, "Let's go!" He walked with a ball-footed prance out of place for his size. When Bob arrived at the water's edge, he looked left, then right, as if making a decision. He glanced back at Rose, winked, and in an unexpected one-eighty twirl, headed north toward Henry's cabin.

Henry
(Sunday)

Henry woke to a dream of Rose. She was walking through his cabin and wore nothing but his blue flannel shirt. He could see the delicate curves of her body. The softness of her hips, the long sweep of her thighs. His shirt held tight to her breasts, falling in pleats from her nipples. He was held captive by her wild green eyes.

Henry forced himself from bed, walked to the bathroom and washed himself awake with cold water, then returned to bed and reached for his notebook.

> I saw you there
> Moonlight in your hair
> Right in front of me
> By the rolling sea
>
> I found you then
> In my dream that night
> You held on to me

Just like the morning light

The muse usually delivered songs to Henry in a stream of words. This song was different. It slipped through Henry, feeling by feeling, holding on to bits of him as he wrote. Vision. Then sensation. The dream of Rose offered up flavors and feelings like sample spoons of ice cream. Just a taste.

He walked shirtless to the piano and glided his hands through the air just above the keys waiting for his fingers to find purchase. For Henry, a melody was a discovered thing. Something unearthed. He would delicately brush away the dust of a song until it revealed itself. His fingers often found the song before his mind had a chance to chime in. Despite his diligence, he could never make a song perfect. But if he wasn't patient, if he rushed it, he could break it. His life was littered with broken songs and once a song was broken, it would never come back. Henry excavated, brushed, and blew the dust from the notes. He hunted for the melody. And when he found the right note, he found a piece of himself.

Henry found one more note that morning. One simple note. It was not a delivered thing. Nothing handed to him by the muse. It was his. That one simple note belonged to him and to Rose. He closed his notebook, stood, walked to the kitchen, and filled the percolator. While the coffee brewed, he padded barefoot to the porch and looked south past his cove. It had been less than ten hours since he and Rose stood on the front porch of her cottage, working through a goodbye like pulling green from a tree. The tide had retreated and was rolling itself onto the shore once more. A fresh canvas of sand and rock. Nonetheless, he scanned the beach hoping to see a sandal print spared by the encouraging waves.

Seeking to find his bearings in caffeine and cold water, Henry pulled the percolator from the burner, poured himself a cup of coffee, retrieved a towel and bar of soap from the bathroom, and walked to Oyster Creek.

> Pull me
> Pull me
> Gravity
> Gravity

Henry set his coffee on a rock near the bank of the creek, took a deep breath, then stepped into the cold water. The flow of Oyster Creek shot daggers through his body and cleared his mind of anything but survival. He puffed out air like a bellow until he was completely submerged, then he stood and lathered his body. As he acclimated to the water, his mind stubbornly returned to Rose. He looked up, into the cedar canopy, and felt a crack along the cornice of his soul. Then, with one more breath, an avalanche that made visible the bare and certain landscape of his heart. *Such is life,* he mused, that the soul should seem blind to circumstance. He recalled a passage from Rumi and recited it out loud as he watched the cedar boughs cross and uncross their long arms in the wind.

> Out beyond ideas of wrongdoing and rightdoing,
> There is a field. I'll meet you there.
> When the soul lies down in that grass,
> The world is too full to talk about.
> Ideas, language, even the phrase *each other*
> Doesn't make any sense.

He thought about his body melting into Rose's in Rumi's field, like the orange and blue of a sunset, creating a new color, beyond language, and uniquely them.

The Invitation

Henry dressed in his work clothes and made his way to the roof of the cabin. It was a hot day for September and he wanted to be done with the shingle work before he walked to meet Rose at high tide. Just as the sun crested the trees to the east of the cabin, he saw a small group of people walking toward the low tide riverlet of Oyster Creek. The group huddled at the creek as a large man at the front of the entourage jumped gingerly across one of the deeper threads of water. Henry had seen the man in town before. He was hard to miss with his long beard and loud laugh.

The man pointed to the creek and then up to Spectacle who squawked while banking large circles in the blue sky. Henry ran his eyes farther down the beach and saw Rose. He stood and wiped the sweat from his brow as he walked to the edge of the roof and watched Rose move smoothly over the beach to join the rest of the group. Despite their short time together, there was a familiarity in her gait and he could tell it was her despite the distance. The swing of her arm and the sway of her hips felt like a known thing, an enchanted memory.

The bearded man stopped in front of the cabin and yelled up to Henry. His jovial tone echoed through the cove.

"HELLOOOO!" The man on the beach cupped his hands over his mouth and continued. "I'm Feather Beard!"

Henry looked confused. "What?"

The man repeated himself. "Feather Beard!" The man grabbed the feather in his beard and wiggled it from side to side.

"Father Bird?" Henry asked.

The man put both his hands on his knees and bent over laughing. "Yes! Exactly!"

Bob put his elbows out to his side and flapped his arms as he walked in a circle. Rose felt like an embarrassed teenager as she watched the performance.

Bob gained his composure and yelled up to Henry again. "I am Father Bird, Feather Beard, we live just down the beach and Mother Bird would like to have you for dinner!"

Rose put her head in her hands.

"What?" Henry yelled back, wondering what he had missed.

Finally, Rose called up to Henry, "Dinner! I think he is asking if you want to come join us for dinner tonight."

Henry smiled wide when he put it all together. "Oh! Sure. That sounds good."

Bob yelled up to Henry, "Come down to our place at seven!"

Feather Beard danced a little jig, spitting mud up from beneath his sandals. Then, without missing a beat, he turned north and marched the group past Henry's cabin to a particularly large glacial erratic that sat on the beach.

Fifteen minutes later, the group passed Henry's cabin on their return journey. He waved as they passed. Rose was the only one to wave back. Her arm was slow to move as she took in the contours of his sweat-drenched chest. Again, Rose found herself wanting to sketch the scene. The shirtless man on top of his cabin. Hammer in hand. His hair was a wild mess. Sweat rimmed the waist of his jeans. Rose pulled her gaze from Henry to find Bob looking back at her with a grin and twinkling eye.

When the group returned to the Island House, Feather Beard gathered them under a shade tree for a final word. A kingfisher chattered from a madrone as Bob shared his thoughts about the geology of the island.

"As you can see, this is one of the most beautiful places in the world for an artist to find inspiration."

As Feather Beard spoke, Rose's mind returned to the conversation she and Henry shared the night before. Henry's eyes held hers as she talked. He asked questions as if looking for the truth of who she was. She felt from Henry a curiosity about her, a wanting to know her, that she had never felt from Simon. She felt Henry softly turning over the stones of her soul and searching the hidden places where true recognition lay.

Rose's attention returned to Feather Beard as he danced from side to side, mimicking the tidal flow that caused the sandstone cliffs near the Island House to erode over time.

"Woosh and woosh and woosh," Feather Beard said as he sprung from one foot to the other. "The dance of life. Can you feel it? Let's all try!"

Feather Beard motioned to the group and they all rocked from one foot to the other as if they were the tide. He looked out over the water as he swayed, his big smile forcing his eyes shut.

The Falls

The tide was halfway up the beach when Rose made it back to her cottage. She lay down on the bed and savored the quiet. Just the sound of approaching waves and a distant cry of a gull.

She closed her eyes and envisioned Henry on the roof of the cabin. She pictured herself inside the cabin, listening to his footsteps through the ceiling. She thought of him finishing his work and descending the ladder onto the porch. She would greet him. Hold him. Smell the sweat on his neck and feel the wet of work through his shirt. They would shower together, eat lunch together, and drive to the store. They would do the beautiful, small, everyday things.

Rose leaned back on her bed and imagined flying high above herself. She looked west to Alder Island, two quarter moons in a sea of blue. She turned then, the landscape sliding by, till she was looking east, to Spokane. East to Simon, Ada, Anna, and Alex.

She thought of Simon's hand in one of hers, soft and familiar. She thought of Henry's hand in the other. New and desirous, and with small calluses where the fingers met the palm. The hand with calluses felt more like home than the soft hand ever did. She thought of letting go of both hands.

She looked west again to the sun setting over the island. Glowing. Then she was glowing. Glowing like the afternoon light in Rome. Glowing in her heart. She was holding no one's hand. She was illuminated. She was flying alone.

I must stop this. This type of glowing is not safe for the ones I love. There is one of me. There are four of them. Four birds in my nest. I will tell Henry. I will go and tell him I can't go to the waterfall. I will tell him he should not come to dinner. Then I will tell him with my eyes that I stopped loving my husband years ago. I will tell him with my eyes that he makes me feel more at home than Simon ever did. I will tell him with my words that my family needs me, and he is not my family. I am falling for him and that is not okay, and we must call it here.

Rose took the initiative to meet Henry at his cabin rather than wait for him to appear at her cottage. Meeting Henry on her terms gave her a feeling of control, and admittedly, she did not want Henry traipsing along the front lawn of the bed-and-breakfast again. She was already dealing with Bob's raised eyebrows and Gail's curious glances.

She reached for the hiking stick Henry had fashioned the night before and headed for the gap in the brambles that led to

Kingfisher Lane. She cleared the cobwebs from the trail and then walked up the lane, making for the footpath that led to Henry's cabin. She would keep her words simple. She tried them aloud as she walked.

"I'm sorry. I can't walk with you. I can't go to the falls. I need to not do that. For so many reasons, I need to not do that. I hope you understand." *He would understand*, she thought. *Henry will understand. He won't make me say more.*

As Rose rounded the third switchback on the trail down to the cabin, she saw Henry in the outdoor shower through yellowing leaves, his tanned back turned to her, water running over his body. He was leaning forward with his left hand against the cabin shingles. His right shoulder flexed. The muscles appearing, then retreating. She watched the water fall with the movement of his right forearm, the muscles rising and falling like piano keys under his skin. She took a step back on the trail and held her breath as the water ran in smooth currents over the tan line that separated his waist from the round of his hips. She could smell his soap. She could hear the water splashing in patterns on the porch. She squeezed her thighs together, feeling overrun by the scene. The small cabin in the midday light. The naked man. Without thinking she crouched down, not wanting to be discovered. She reached forward and moved a fern with her fingers to clear the view. She let the fern snap back into place when she saw the muscles along Henry's shoulders clench hard and then release. His breath deepened. His head slipped back and in a low voice, he whispered her name.

Rose snuck back up the trail to Kingfisher Lane like a wild thing, hunched and light-footed. As she crested the top of the trail, she heard the cabin door slam shut. She stood at the top of the trail looking down the lane. Her heart raced. She was surprised by her voyeurism. She put a hand on Henry's mailbox as her body filled with competing emotions–a mixture of arousal and shame. She looked in the direction of her cottage, then back to the cabin, then lifted her hand from the mailbox and walked slowly back down the lane.

Rose sat on a log overlooking the water at the bottom of the road and looked out over the high tide. She knew Henry would be along shortly and she listened for the crunch of gravel from beyond the bend in the road. When at last she heard Henry's footsteps, she stood and walked up the road to meet him.

Henry smiled when he saw her. "I was just coming to get you!"

Rose leaned on the hiking stick. "I figured I'd beat you to it."

Henry's hair was wet from the shower and he smelled of the soap that had drifted up the trail to greet her as she watched him. "I'm glad you brought the hiking stick! We will have some nettles to clear on the trail to the falls. I haven't been up there in thirty years; it may be a jungle expedition."

Rose lifted the hiking stick into the air like a warrior. "Adventure!"

Henry smiled. "I love your sense of adventure, Rose."

Rose leaned on the stick again. The muscles of her arm flexed. She took a deep breath. Henry held her with his eyes. She felt the empty places open. She felt a dam crack and a river rush in to fill the void. She felt whole. She felt herself. She took a breath and opened her mouth to speak. Rose did not say the words that she tested. They were no longer there.

Henry raised a brow and smiled at her. He did not know the proper greeting. A hug seemed too familiar and a handshake seemed overly formal.

"Well, onward!" Henry said as he turned and led the way up the lane.

They walked together along the lane until they came to the small bridge that spanned Oyster Creek. Henry pointed to a thin game trail that ran along the north side of the creek.

"That's our trail. Looks like the deer have done some of the work for us."

Henry talked over his shoulder as they walked, asking questions and stopping on occasion to point out a natural landmark that held a memory from his childhood. "I would sit there next to the creek and play my guitar for hours. I'd try to match the babble and tone of the water." And a bit farther on, "I would sit under that alder and play on rainy days."

Then, Henry's attention was on her again. His soft questions.

"Tell me more about your art."

"When do you paint?"

"What do you feel when you paint?"

"Where do you most like to paint?"

After each question was answered, they would walk quietly as Henry committed the nuance of Rose's answers to memory. He wanted to know the geography of her. He wanted to understand the delicate intricacies of her mind. After a mile of walking, they found themselves in comfortable silence, their proximity to one another in the secluded valley filling their souls.

Henry pointed up the trail to a section of steep switchbacks that weaved through a garden of granite boulders. The trail disappeared into a thicket of nettles before re-emerging on the other side of the boulder field.

"May I?" Henry asked, nodding to Rose's hiking stick.

"No way! I got this," Rose said as she sidestepped Henry and worked her way through the nettles swinging the hiking stick like a scythe. Henry watched her mow down the tall plants with graceful strokes. Her long legs pushed forward until the nettles lay in a path of submission.

"Well done!" Henry said. Then he nodded to a red welt rising up on her calf. "Looks like one of them got you."

Rose grinned. "That just means I'm doing it right. They wanted a sacrifice."

Just then, a breeze blew down the valley, teasing Rose's hair and bringing with it the sound of the falls.

"Not far now," Henry said as they walked together, rounding the bend in lockstep. A cool mist from the waterfall settled over them as they took in the view. Henry pointed across the pool to a sunny spot on a gravel bar near the bottom of the falls. "That's our spot. Just there. Out of the breeze. We may need to swim for it though."

A smile stretched across Rose's face, and before Henry could react, she had slipped off her denim shorts and shirt. Her legs left wakes in the water. Her sports bra was dark from sweat. She waded into the water until she was thigh deep, then she dove into the pool and swam with long strokes to the other side. Henry followed Rose's lead, stripping off his shirt and walking carefully across the sharp rocks with his hands out to his sides for balance. The muscles of his stomach tightened and released with each step.

"Jump in, tenderfoot!" Rose yelled.

Henry leapt and splashed into the water. He opened his eyes when he was fully submerged and saw that the pool was full of salmon waiting to scale the falls. Henry surfaced next to Rose and wiped the water from his face.

"We're not alone," Henry said, nodding to the pool. "I'd say there are about fifty coho down there. It's not going to rain much today. How about we give them a hand?"

Henry waded just below the falls, bent down into the water, and lifted a writhing salmon from the depths. He took a step up into the cascade of water.

"Good luck, my friend!" Henry said to the salmon as he let it go over the top lip of the falls. "One down! Come on, give me a hand."

Rose waded to where Henry stood.

"Okay, your turn," Henry said.

Rose knelt down and scooped a salmon out of the water, its muscles tight in her hands.

"Oh my god, it's beautiful," Rose said as she held the fish, gazing into its dark searching eyes.

"Hand it up here."

Rose handed Henry the salmon and he eased it up over the lip of the falls.

When he looked back at Rose, she had another fish in her hands. The silver-sided creature bucked from side to side, splashing water onto her face. Her dark hair was in tangles over her slender shoulders. Her sports bra edged down slightly by the falling water, revealing a faint tanline. She smiled up at him and Henry felt his heart locking into a truth as primitive and unyielding as the fish in her hands. He realized, at that moment, that he would never be the same. Something had been revealed to him. An awareness that days before was unknown. This was his woman. There was no other. And he felt a tear in his soul, as if something was leaving him and then being replaced by a force far greater. A known thing. An answer to a question. It was her. In all the ways, it was her.

"Are you going to take it?" Rose yelled through the mist.

"What?"

"The fish!" Rose yelled. "Are you going to take the fish?"

"Right! Yes, of course."

Henry reached down and took the salmon from Rose's hands. And as he slid the fish over the falls, he became aware of the fact that he loved Rose. That he always would, however foolish it was. That sometimes life was cruel in what it showed you, only to take it away. But he would much rather know what his heart was capable of than not know it. *There are some people who are worth heartbreak,* Henry thought.

They sunned themselves as they walked back down the trail, feeling the freedom that came with secluded places. Rose paused on the trail and looked down over Oyster Creek. She felt no pressure or expectation, just the quiet comfort of Henry. She realized she had never felt this way with a man. It was a feeling that she had only found with her closest friends. With Henry, she was able to set aside the weighted veil of judgment, the need for performance, and the pretending that she felt with Simon. She felt like herself. She felt known. She felt loved for everything she was.

Henry and Rose were deep in conversation when they arrived at the bridge on Kingfisher Lane.

"Can I walk you back to your cottage?"

"No, that's okay. I've got it. I feel like a superhero with this," Rose said as she lifted the hiking stick.

"You certainly look the part." Henry said.

"I'll see you at dinner tonight?"

"Of course. I'd hate to disappoint Father Bird."

Rose corrected him. "Feather Beard."

"Right," Henry said, "Feather Beard. I'll walk you to the end of the lane, then."

"Very well," Rose acquiesced.

When they reached the path through the woods at the end of Kingfisher Lane, Rose stopped and leaned on her hiking stick.

"Thanks for the adventure."

"Anytime."

A quiet moment. The pull of each other.

"See you tonight."

"Yes, see you tonight."

Rose could feel Henry's eyes on her as she rounded the bend in the trail. She liked knowing that he was watching. She liked knowing that if she turned she would see him looking after her.

Leaping

Rose pulled the green dress from her backpack and laid it over the shower rod in the hope that the steam would smooth out the wrinkles. The dress was a cotton blend with just enough stretch to reveal her soft curves. *Beautiful, and just shy of suggestive,* she thought.

She slipped the dress on quickly after her shower, allowing it to dry while she walked through the cottage. The dress matched her eyes and she applied a thin layer of mascara to accentuate the point. Her eyes were her favorite feature. Persian, perhaps. A remnant of an Arabian love affair somewhere in her gene pool.

Bob had placed a long teak table on the flagstone patio just above the beach. The patio ran the length of the house and its proximity to the water gave diners the feeling of being on a ship at sea. The breaking waves created a soft mist that held in the air.

Rose was watching a porpoise play in the wake of a sailboat when Gail walked up beside her.

"It's beautiful now," Gail said, "but every winter this patio becomes the most terrifying place on earth. Tempests blow in from the north and create ocean-sized swells. Whenever that happens, I make Feather Beard sit on the patio in his slicker and fishing waders to keep an eye out for rogue waves that might send driftwood over the bulkhead. Last year, we had to build a three-foot wall of sandbags along the perimeter of the patio to keep the water out of the house. But all the fuss is worth it. In the summer,"—Gail paused as she saw Henry walking up the stairs to the patio—"it's pure beauty."

Gail moved across the flagstones at a startling speed. "Welcome to the Island House!" Gail said, breathless and with a bead of sweat surfacing on her forehead. "Finally, I get to meet our neighbor!"

Henry held out his hand but Gail brushed it aside and hugged him. She took her time with the hug, assessing the strength of his back through his denim shirt. Henry felt as if he were being appraised for a livestock auction.

"Now you, my dear, are a specimen."

Henry took a step back as Bob approached.

"I don't see what all the fuss is about! Just because he looks like one of those fellas on the cover of those smut books you buy at the Thriftway doesn't mean we have to stand here ogling. Come on this way, Hank. You like whiskey, right?"

Henry caught Rose's eye and shrugged as Bob guided him into the house. When he reappeared, he held a tumbler of whiskey in his hand. "Is this seat taken?"

Rose edged to the side. "It is now."

Henry sat his whiskey on the table. "That man knows his whiskey," Henry said. "Here, try this."

Henry handed Rose the tumbler. She watched the muscles of his forearms move as he gripped the glass and thought back to seeing him in the outside shower. She readjusted herself on the seat and took a sip from Henry's glass. The whiskey stung Rose's lips, then slid warm and smooth over her tongue.

"It tastes like it was made by an artist," Rose said.

"I suppose that's fitting. We are at art camp, after all," Henry said.

Rose looked at the other two guests. "I guess that's true, although I'm starting to think this is all just a ruse for people to get together and drink."

"That's a pretty good idea, actually." Henry was mid-sentence when a salmon leapt from the water ten yards from the beach. The group turned to see the fish leap two more times. Rose looked at Henry.

"We may have some more work to do tomorrow?"

Bob interjected from behind, with loud clapping. "They're back! They came back!"

Gail appeared from the lodge with a kitchen towel over her shoulder just in time to see another wild leap. She slapped her thigh with an open palm.

"Hot damn, it's officially fall!"

Just then, another fish leapt out of the water and landed with a slap. Rose smiled at the excitement. She had always measured seasons by the changing light, or the falling of leaves, never by leaping fish.

Rose looked to Henry, admiring his thoughtful expression. "What are you thinking about?"

"I'm thinking I feel like one of those salmon."

"How so?"

"I feel like I've come home. It's an ease in my heart."

"I can see how this island would make you feel that." Rose put her hand on Henry's forearm.

"It's not just the island."

Rose moved her hand back to her side. "What else is it?"

"It's you. You are familiar to me. Your soul. We have known each other, I think."

Rose looked away and cleared her throat, then looked at Henry with soft eyes.

Henry took a breath.

"You know what I like about you, Rose?" Henry asked. "I like how curious you are. You ask questions. People don't do that very often. Most of the world is so consumed in their own suffering that they don't ask about anyone else's." Henry smiled. "It's just a sea of telling."

Rose was never completely comfortable with compliments, but Henry's rang true and she felt it deeply. She put her hand on Henry's forearm. The edge of her lips turned up in a coy smile.

"I'm happy to help you suffer, Henry."

After a dessert of blackberry cobbler, Henry took the lead on clearing dishes. He thanked Gail and Bob for the meal and promised to come by more often. It was the appropriate time to head home, but the pull of Rose kept Henry lingering. He said one more round of goodbyes, stalling, then worked his way across the patio and down to the beach. Rose called out after him.

"Hey, let me walk you back. I don't want you to get lost."

Henry turned and looked up from the beach. The sun on her face. Henry lost his words then found them again. "I was beginning to feel a bit turned around."

"Thank god I said something! It's this way," Rose said as she jumped from the bulkhead and down to the beach. She began walking in the opposite direction of Henry's cabin.

"You know, that doesn't feel quite right, but I'm going to trust my gut on this and follow you," Henry said.

Rose laughed and turned to face him. She pointed in the direction of his cabin, then set off with Henry trailing behind. He watched the movement of her body as she walked. The delicate sway of her hips drew the breath from his chest. Henry swept his eyes over Rose's rounded hips and his mind emptied of rational thought. *Art*, Henry thought. He saw eons of creation in the way her hips rolled. Her rhythmic movement like the melody of some ancient music.

> Move with me
> You beautiful light
> Move with me tonight
>
> Let me watch you
> Let me see you
> Move with me

He wanted to run his hands along the edges of her. He wanted to close his eyes and feel the movement of her body. He wanted to know the mechanics of her, as if understanding how she moved would placate a carnal curiosity.

Rose looked back and caught the sweep of Henry's eyes. She felt a flash of modesty that was quickly overruled by the warmth of being desired. There was something animal bubbling up inside her. She felt it on the hike as she swam. She felt it when she watched Henry in the shower. She felt it in Henry's eyes, his softness wrapped in strength, the simple, easy flow of their conversation. The slow burn of his glances created a powerful current, like a river rounding a bend. Rose wanted to jump in and let it wash over her. Let it take her all the way to the sea.

Rose looked out over the water as they walked, feeling like she was simply part of the natural movement of things. That this connection, however fleeting, was kindled somewhere ancient. A natural thing. A carved fjord. A glacial erratic dropped in place ages ago.

Henry stopped when they arrived at the sandy, low-tide fingers of Oyster Creek. The creek was a natural barrier between where the evening wanted to take itself and the realities of their circumstance. They stilled at the creek's edge and listened to the liquid babble, both of them feeling the pull of each other.

Henry stepped into the creek then looked to Rose. "You know the way back?"

"No clue, but I'm feeling *that* way." Rose nodded in the direction they had come. Henry pointed up to the cloud-soaked sky.

"Just follow the stars."

Rose looked up at the blanket of darkness. "Good advice."

"Can I take you fishing tomorrow? I'll pick you up at high tide?" The offer felt hurried. Forced. *Relax*, he thought.

"Yes. High tide," Rose said. Feeling, not thinking.

They quieted. Felt the tug of each other again. A listening moment. And as they stood in the cool, quiet world, the beach came to life around them. The sound of clams and oysters, shore crabs, and sculpins, all part of the succulent smacking of the living earth. Spurts of pleasure followed by retreat. Everything wanting its chance to live. Henry rocked back and forth on his boot. Leaning toward the cabin then toward Rose. A pendulum of consciousness. He took another step into the creek.

"Good night, Rose."

"Good night, Henry."

Rose
(Monday)

Rose lay in bed watching the rain bead up on the bay window. Her eyes caught on an individual raindrop and she watched as the drop grew in size until its weight broke the surface tension, sending it down the window. Raindrops racing raindrops to the earth. Rose rolled from bed and took inventory of her emotions as she walked to the window. No matter the circumstances surrounding her life, anxiety always found her in the morning. But for reasons she could not identify, she felt calm and relaxed. She slid on her jeans, then worked her arms through her hooded sweatshirt. *Coffee*, she thought. *I need coffee.* Breakfast would not be ready for an hour. Plenty of time for a cup.

    She found Feather Beard next to the fireplace, hunkered over a pile of kindling, looking very much like an end-of-season mall Santa in dirty sweats. He lit a ball of newspaper with one hand while holding his beard away from the flame with the other. He was so engrossed in the task at hand that he was unaware of the generous length of butt crack that climbed like a crag from his elastic waistband. He puffed his chest, broadened his shoulders, and gave the fire a spirited blow. When the fire caught, he stood from his crouch like an unsure toddler. Once his legs were under him, he straightened himself, put his hands on his waist, and pushed his vertebrae back into place.

"Good morning!" Feather Beard said. "You've found me at my finest this morning, Wild Rose." He shuffled his feet into a little dance. "Still got it." He brushed the bark off the front of his shirt. "Did you sleep well?"

"Very well, thank you."

Feather Beard strutted past Rose toward the kitchen. He called over his shoulder, "Coffee's on the table! Help yourself. It's from the Island Roasters. Not that burned-up, corporate shit."

Bob disappeared into the kitchen, letting the door slap shut behind him. Rose heard a spank followed by a cackle from Gail, then Feather Beard's low voice, "Are you and that fine ass of yours done with breakfast?"

Rose helped herself to coffee and returned to the fire with a steaming cup in hand. She looked through the bookshelf next to the fireplace and found an anthology of poems. She took the book to the couch, flipped through the pages, and landed on "The Summer Day" by Mary Oliver. *Mary always seems to find me when I'm looking for answers*, Rose thought. She ran her finger over the final line and read aloud, "Tell me, what is it you plan to do with your one wild and precious life?" Rose repeated the line, the question filling her. She was about to repeat the line a second time when Gail walked into the great room and sat down on the couch next to her. Rose's coffee sloshed, leaving dark drips on her jeans. Gail seemed not to notice.

"The mountain was out yesterday," Gail proclaimed.

Rose looked up, trying to make sense of the announcement.

"It's not always out–the mountain. It's often covered in clouds, but every once in a while she shines bright in all her glory." Gail fanned her hands out in front of her as she spoke. "Bob and I drove into town yesterday and on the way back we decided to mosey over to the east side of the island and see if she was out, and there she was. It never gets old looking at her."

Rose put her book down. "Do you mean Mount Rainier?"

Gail laughed and slapped her hip. Another splash of coffee landed on Rose's pants.

"Of course I mean Mount Rainier. You eastsiders don't know the magic of that mountain. Here on the island, we have two types of days: there are days when the mountain is out and there are days when it is not."

Rose gave Gail a smile. "Well, excuse me for my simple-minded 'eastsider' confusion."

Rose opened her book again, hoping Gail would take the cue and end the conversation.

Gail said, "You know, I climbed it once."

Rose set her book down again. "Really?"

Gail ran her hands over her rounded stomach. "I was not always so womanly," she said, sticking her chest out and making a show of her proportions. She pointed at herself with a thick thumb. "I climbed every one of those 14,440 feet right up to the top. I shit you not."

Gail stood and waddled over to the fireplace, retrieved a framed photo and handed it to Rose. Rose looked down at a beautiful young woman with a rope around her waist and an ice ax in her hand. The woman in the photo wore Gail's same gap-toothed smile.

"You look like a model in an adventure magazine."

Gail smiled, reached down and took the picture back. She wiped the glass with her apron and sat back down on the couch.

"My family moved to Alder Island when I was a little girl. My father got a job as a flight engineer at Boeing and my mother wanted a house where she could look out and see America. We ended up on the east side of the island with a wide-open view of Mount Rainier. I spent my whole life looking up at that mountain. One day, I decided that I wanted to be up there looking down here. So I started making my plans. My dad said I was crazy and I should leave the mountain climbing to my brothers. 'Gailie girl,' he would say, 'I'll be damned if I let you climb that mountain!' My mom was no help.

She just shook her head and said, 'You're being foolish. Girls don't climb mountains.'"

Gail's eyes narrowed and she leaned in toward Rose. "But I saw something in my mom's eyes that I did not see in my father's. Something like a challenge. She would do that, my mom, challenge me with her eyes to follow an idea. Her challenge was always in her eyes. Never in her words. And right then, I decided that I was going to climb that mountain just for me. I started training in the mornings and reading books about mountain climbing at night. I think my mom knew what I was up to but she never said a word. And then one day, when I was seventeen, I convinced my parents to let me spend a week off the island with my friend who was going to college at the University of Puget Sound. It was the only big lie I ever told my parents. When I got to my friend's apartment, I borrowed her car, drove up to Paradise on Mount Rainier, and I went for it. I ended up connecting with another group of climbers, thank god, and I made it to the summit. And when I was up there, I looked down here and I knew what down here looked like from up there. It's hard to explain, but I just needed to know. I was sunburnt and red as a boiled crab when I got home and I'm pretty sure my mom knew what I had done."

Gail walked back to the fireplace and put the picture back on the mantel. "You've got to live for you, Rose. I know life has its responsibilities and those are important to manage, but I'm glad I climbed that mountain. I'm glad I know what down here looks like from up there." Gail winked at Rose. "Be wild. Even if only for a moment. Be wild."

Rose put her book down and let the words settle in. She thought of the adventures she longed to have. The life she longed to live. She thought about loving, even for a moment. She thought about Henry. Rose looked out the open door onto the porch. Cool air came through the door and teased at her hair. She felt an ache of longing for her children and a pull of longing for herself and her wild nature. Her one wild and precious life.

Fish On

It was a twenty-minute drive from the cabin to the fishing beach on the southwest side of the island. Henry worked Frank's gears through the ten miles of hairpin turns and gravel roads between his cabin and the best-kept secret on the island. His fingers bounced along on the stick shift with each bump in the road. The sound of Henry's voice, the hum of Frank's engine, and the cool breeze held a nostalgic familiarity to Rose, and as they rounded a sharp turn, Rose realized that the familiarity was not with the setting but within herself. She found herself returning to the adventurous spirit that, over time, had settled just below her consciousness.

She realized in that moment that she was coming home–not to the world around her, but to the world within her. A comfort. A yes. A this. She looked through the dirty windshield with fresh eyes, as if something had been returned to her. The adventurer, the explorer, the artist. The self who was not mired in Simon's expectations of what she should be, but instead the self that she simply was. As Henry brought Frank to a stop in front of a pile of storm-blown driftwood, Rose was smiling.

"Here we are," Henry said as he turned to Rose. "You look happy."

"I am."

Henry retrieved the fly rod from the back seat and threaded the floating line through its guides as Rose stood by his side watching the movement of his hands. He made small adjustments as he worked the line through the holes. Each guide required more delicate finger work. Rose leaned back and rested on Frank's door as Henry sang to himself.

> Thread my life
> One eye at a time
> Thread my life
> Down the center line
>
> One way to go
> One place to be
> Thread my life
> You through me

Rose leaned into her feelings trying to figure out what to do about this man that felt like a long-lost friend. She wondered about the vibration of emotion teasing up from the deep parts of her.

"Thread my life." Rose repeated aloud the words that Henry had sung. "Thread my life, you through me."

She smiled at the sound of Henry's voice and how he felt comfortable enough to sing with her nearby. She liked the way he shared his thoughts, not as some ego-fueled measure of intellect, but instead as a sharing of the curious world.

"There is a drop-off about twenty yards out." Henry pointed beyond a group of widgeons that bobbed in the waves preening themselves. A salmon jumped, frightening the birds, and they drummed their wings as they lifted off the water in a cloud of vapor.

"That's our spot." Henry nodded to the ripples where the fish had landed. He looked out over the water and pointed to a piece of floating driftwood. "Slack tide. We timed this perfectly."

Rose followed Henry over to the driftwood berm and down to the beach. She was wearing her cutoff jean shorts, flip-flops, and a gray fleece jacket. She liked the way the fleece held her body. Warm and snug to her curves. She never associated a fleece jacket with feeling beautiful, but the cut of it suited her, and the fullness of her athletic body felt alive.

Rose scaled the driftwood berm and followed Henry out to the gravel point on the beach. She felt the movement of her body as she walked and compared her movement to Henry's narrow-hipped strides. Even the way Henry moved felt familiar to her, as if they had walked a thousand miles together on some distant trail.

Henry looked back to Rose. The sun ran through her hair, creating a halo of filtered light. The edges of her body were framed with a soft glow. Henry selfishly took her in. He thought back through the beautiful moments of his life. The sun setting from the summit of Mount Baker. The northern lights above the cabin when he was a boy. Despite his effort, he could not recall a more beautiful scene than Rose in the afternoon light. Her profile, the angle of her jaw, the strength in her legs. Henry thought of music. The notes he had played and the words he had written. There was no way to capture what he saw. She was the perfect song.

Rose stood a few feet from Henry and, in that moment, she knew what it felt like to be fully seen and hungered for. She held Henry's eyes and watched him take her in. And instead of retreating, instead of looking away and being bashful, she met his gaze and felt the truth of him fill her soul. A fish jumped, waves crashed, the world muted and slowed.

"Fishing," Rose said.

Henry smiled, returning to himself. "Fishing."

Henry waded through the shallows, then stopped abruptly and tested the sand with his foot. He took another step and submerged into thigh-deep water.

"I think we found the drop-off."

Henry took a step back and unhooked the fly from the quark. He drew the rod back and let the line roll out behind him. A flash of silver in the sunlight. Then he swung the rod forward. The fly switched directions and drifted out toward the rings in the water. Henry repeated the motion and let the line unfurl behind him. He looked back to Rose as the line stretched to its full length and then he whipped it forward once more. When the fly landed, Henry crouched forward and pulled the line back a few inches at a time. His attention focused as he made the fly come alive. Water flew from the reel when Henry stripped the line, creating a rainbow of mist.

He sensed the fish before it struck. His eyes narrowed. The rod tip bent. The line tightened. The salmon leapt out of the water and bucked in the air. Rose clapped her hands as she watched the fish run. The reel buzzed and the fish jumped again, this time farther offshore. Its silver sides glistened in the sunlight as it leapt a third time.

Henry yelled over his shoulder to Rose. "Come over here! Take the rod."

Rose splashed through the water toward Henry, laughing.

"If he runs, let him run."

Rose's heart pounded as she took the rod in her hands. "I've never done this before, Henry!"

Henry smiled. "Perfect!" He circled behind her and spoke softly in her ear. "All right, let it run."

Rose let the fish take the line.

"Okay, now, reel in. Yes, Rose."

She felt the warmth of Henry's breath on her neck. The vibration of his voice in her ear.

Henry reached an arm around her and put his left hand over hers. He pulled the rod up. "There. Just like that."

As Rose raised the rod tip, Henry kept his hand on hers and lifted the rod higher.

"Okay, now reel in the slack."

Rose reeled as the rod settled. Henry pulled up one more time and again Rose reeled. "Perfect. Just like that."

Rose felt her skin tingle as Henry slid his hands from hers and took a step back. She pulled the rod tip up and reeled again.

"That's great, Rose, just like that."

After fifteen minutes, the fish was run out and swam slowly on its side by Rose's feet.

"Bring her in just a little closer to me."

Rose guided the fish into the shallows as Henry knelt down on one knee and ran his hands under the fish's belly. Water dripped from his flannel shirt sleeves as Henry slowly lifted the fish, holding it tightly as it writhed, and then delicately as it became still in his hands. He waded in close to Rose.

"It's beautiful!" Rose said as she took the weight of the sleek, rounded body. She could feel every muscle in the fish flex and relax.

"Let's let her go," Henry said.

Rose leaned the fish into the water and Henry steadied it. They loosened their grip and watched the fish flash into the depths.

"That was exhilarating!" Rose exclaimed.

"Such is life," Henry said.

They walked back to the beach together and sat down on a sun-bleached log. Rose reached down and grabbed a stick from the beach and drew the roofline of Henry's cabin.

"That's pretty good, actually."

Rose looked up at Henry and smiled. "Thank you. I meant to bring my sketch pad but the beach will have to do. I used to draw all the time."

"What changed?" Henry asked.

"Life, I guess. And I haven't felt like painting in quite some time. But there is something about this place, or maybe my state of mind, that is calling me back to it."

"You're an artist. I see it."

"Yes, I'm an artist."

Henry crouched down next to the drawing and put a small rock on the roof of the cabin. "When I was a kid I would sit up here on the roof and watch the sunset." He drew a faint line from the roof to the north side of the cabin. "I would look up into the woods just as the sun disappeared behind the Olympics. There is a grove of madrone trees, right here." Henry drew a circle in the sand north of the cabin. "Just after the sunset, the red bark would glow and dance and I felt something transcendent in it all. As if the trees were telling me something about truth and life."

"What is the truth, Henry?"

Henry leaned back.

"I guess the truth is that there are more lessons about life in that stand of madrones at sunset than in all the books of the world. I think nature is always communicating, telling us things, and the right light helps us see it."

Rose set her elbow on Henry's shoulder. It felt natural to touch him. He fit. Like a beloved T-shirt. So familiar in just the right way.

Rose watched as Henry unthreaded the line through the fly rod. She lost herself in the movement of his fingers. She liked how noticing little things about him made her feel. A chip on his thumb nail, the way the hair from his arm lightened as it moved on to his hand.

As Henry placed the fly rod in the back of Frank, Rose took a step toward him. She felt pulled and unaware of herself. Henry looked up and held her eye.

"I, um… I…thank you for–" she reached out and put a hand on his cheek. She ran her hand behind his head and kissed him with soft lips. The sensation of his lips filled her body as if she had kissed all of him and he had kissed all of her.

Henry breathed in deep when she pulled back.

"Shit! I'm sorry," Rose said, "I don't know why I--"

Henry moved a stray hair from in front of Rose's eye. "You are alive and radiant and beautiful."

Rose felt a wash of guilt as she walked to the passenger door and sat down in Frank. They drove in silence as Henry maneuvered Frank through the winding roads back to the Island House. Rose's heart wrestled with her consciousness, creating waves of anxiety that smashed into her heart. Her mind returned to home, feeling a need to ground herself in the voices of those she loved. As they crested a hill on the east side of the island, Rose reached into her backpack and fished out her cell phone. It had been three days since Rose had spoken to Simon and the kids. There was no reception at the Island House and she felt a mix of guilt and relief when she saw Simon's name come up on her cell phone's voicemail. Rose listened to the message, then looked to Henry. "I need to make a call. Could you pull over up here?"

"Of course," Henry said as he pulled Frank into an overlook.

Rose dialed home and put the phone to her ear as the Land Cruiser came to a stop. "HEY, MOM!" All three of her children's voices rang through the receiver.

"Hey, babies!" Rose answered with a new tone, a sweet softness in her voice. A mothering voice. Henry could not help but feel the depth of his unknowing. Rose the mother. Rose the wife.

This woman, the woman with whom he was drifting into in the present, was not his in the past or the future. Henry gripped the wheel and rolled up his window to quiet the wind noise.

"How are you? I miss you!"

"Mommy! I went to Claire's house and they got a new puppy, and the puppy's name is Oliver, and he has a spot on his eye, and the puppy bit Ella!"

Rose furrowed her brow. "The puppy bit Ella?" Her voice edged with concern.

Then another small voice came on the phone. "He did not bite me, he just put his gross mouth on my hand and scratched me."

Then a boy's voice. "PUPPY! I WANT A PUPPY!"

Rose smiled, "I know you want a puppy, Alex, but no puppies until I see you being nicer to your sisters."

The phone went quiet. Then a man's voice. "Hey, baby! I've been calling but I can't get through. I thought maybe you had run off."

Henry turned the engine off and opened his door. "I'll give you a moment," Henry mouthed as he stepped out of the car and walked to a patch of blackberries.

Rose felt divided as she tried to reconcile two worlds at once. "Yeah! Sorry, the reception here is horrible. This place is a bit wild, and the bed-and-breakfast is down in a cove. It feels isolated from the rest of the world and I kind of love it, if I'm being honest."

"Well, don't love it too much. I need you back here. We're hosting my partners at the house on Thursday and these kids are insane. Damn it, now I've got that P.O.S. anesthesiologist, Edward, calling in. I've got to run. Say goodbye to your mom, kids."

"BYE, MOMMY."

Rose pulled the phone from her ear, feeling an ache for her children and a sting that accompanied most conversations with Simon. He never failed to mention the practical convenience she provided in his life. Never shared his feelings of missing her.

She sat quietly, letting the realities of her life off the island flow over her. She then looked over to Henry, opened the car door, and walked across the gravel to where he stood picking berries. As she approached, Henry extended a handful of blackberries.

"Still a few ripe ones."

She looked down and plucked two berries out of his palm. "That was my family."

Henry cleared his throat. "I hope that's who that was, otherwise you've got a real problem on your hands."

Henry turned and looked over the water to the summer-white peak of Mount Rainier in the distance. A seagull floated up on a thermal and hung in the air over Wayfair Inlet. When he looked back at Rose, his eyes were warm and kind.

"Something special lives here between us, Rose."

Rose looked at her feet, noticing a sliver of dried kelp on her big toe. She took her other foot and brushed it away.

"I don't want to disrupt your life, Rose. These feelings I have for you, I don't need them back, but they are real."

Rose looked at Henry, finding sincerity in his dark brown eyes.

"I've always been someone to follow my dreams, Rose, even if it flows against the expectation. I follow my dreams."

Rose tightened her lips, a wash of panic hammered in her chest. "Why say this, Henry? Why put words to it? Why give it a voice and make it real? I shouldn't have kissed you. I was caught up. It was a mistake."

"I'm not going to pretend, Rose."

Rose felt her eyes water. "That's not fair, Henry. It's not fair for you to say those things to me. You don't…." Rose looked back to the car hoping to find the right words. "You're telling me things I can't have."

Henry hesitated. "I know what I feel and I'm not one to hold my thoughts for fear of offending you. I am not going to live with a closed heart."

Rose turned on her heel and walked back to Frank. She wanted to scream. She wanted to hit the dash and break the truth that was boiling inside her. She wanted to tell the truth to shut the fuck up.

Henry opened the driver's-side door and sat down. The car shifted with his weight. "I know you feel it too, Rose. I'm not going to pretend it away."

Rose sat, her body humming, and stroked the inside of her knee with her thumb. She felt more aligned with this man after two days than she had ever felt with Simon after ten years. Simon always backed down when emotions were involved or turned an argument around so she felt crazy. And here was this man. This beautiful man sharing himself with her and not backing down. Rose's hands began to shake. "Please, Henry. Just drive me back. Please."

Henry turned the ignition and guided Frank back onto the highway. They rode in silence, the space between them feeling like a gear that needed to shift.

It was late afternoon when they arrived back at the Island House. Henry slowed to a stop in front of the house. They sat quietly, listening to the hum of Frank's engine. Rose looked through the windshield, not seeing. Just feeling. She reached for Henry's hand and held it. She brought it to her lips and kissed it, then opened the car door and got out.

Henry
(Tuesday)

Henry woke the next morning with a heavy heart. His mind was clouded in grief as he replayed their conversation in his mind. *Why say anything? Why say anything? Why say anything?* He repeated the words like a mantra as he made coffee and sat down at the piano. He took a deep breath, put his thoughts aside, and began to sing.

>   I saw you there
>   Moonlight in your hair
>   Right in front of me
>   By the rolling sea
>
>   I found you then
>   In my dream that night
>   You held on to me
>   Just like the morning light

I felt you there
Standing next to me
Like water rushing home
To the sea

You're my wild Rose
You're my Ocean Blue
You're the one I chose
I'm in love with you

Rose
(Tuesday)

Rose watched the waves splash along the bulkhead in front of her cottage. The tide was high and the beach between the Island House and Henry's cabin was submerged under six feet of water. Rose had made her decision in the night, giving in to what she wanted. She rolled in bed, warring with her desire to feel fully seen and her responsibility of being fully faithful. Ultimately, her heart and her soul lined up and whispered an answer that lay outside her conscious self.

Rose packed her things into her backpack, grabbed the hiking stick Henry made, and charted a path to the trail through the brambles. Clouds held low in the trees as she walked through the wet grass. Rose saw Gail through the kitchen window washing dishes at the sink. She looked up and caught Rose's eye. A faint smile passed over Gail's face as she turned and disappeared into the kitchen.

The forest had already begun to reclaim the path to Kingfisher Lane and Rose had to swing the maple limb at blackberry bushes and sword ferns to clear the way. Each step brought with it a more profound feeling of resolution. The rain was falling steadily when the trail opened up at the end of the road. Rose paused and listened to the sound of the forest close up behind her. There was no going back. She moved a dripping strand of hair from her face and leaned onto the hiking stick, took a deep breath, then walked up Kingfisher Lane to Henry's cabin.

As she walked, she thought of the moment they shared on the footbridge. The sound of Oyster Creek and the salmon returning. She stopped and closed her eyes and she became a salmon. Each turn in the trail was a rapid she had to navigate on her way home. This was what she wanted. She would love Henry David James and she would be fully seen, if only for a moment.

The sound of piano music mixed with the rain and rushing creek as Rose approached the cabin. The notes were soft and low like wood smoke. She could hear Henry's voice through the rain but the words were unclear. When Rose climbed the steps to the front porch, she saw Henry through the crown-glass panes in the Dutch door. He was sitting at the piano, the muscles of his back moving almost imperceptibly as he played, his head bowed as if praying. Rose watched Henry's right hand move over the keys, calling up the soft whisper of notes. It was a chorus. A love song. The notes drifted. The rain fell. Henry's heart bled and Rose listened. She felt tears run down her cheeks. She felt what he felt. She was lost in him. His vulnerability brought her heart even closer to his and she melted into him as he played. She claimed him. Her heart opened, pulled him in, then weaved back together like the forest claiming the trail.

Hello in There

Henry wept for the first time in years and he let the tears roll down his cheeks like the rain on the windows. When the notes had run through him, he rested his fingers on the keys and played two notes over and over in time with the rain tapping on the chimney flashing. He noticed another tap. Something softer. Something out of beat. Henry turned to see Rose standing outside the door, one finger tapping on the glass. Her dark hair hung wet and loose from her shoulders.

Henry stared at her. An apparition from the forest. Rose tapped again, breaking his trance. He ran his forearm across his cheeks and walked to the door.

"Hi," she mouthed through the glass.

Henry opened the door, reached to her, and cupped his warm hands on her cool cheeks. Rose lifted her hands and wrapped her fingers around his forearms.

"Hi," Henry said. Then he kissed her soft like a feather.

Henry took Rose's pack from her shoulder and set it inside the door beside his work boots. He looked down at the pack, appreciating the sight of having part of her in his space. A small thing that gave her ownership of the cabin. He wanted his place to be her place. He wanted her to claim it, to feel at home in the little cabin by the sea. Maybe it could be hers. Maybe it could be theirs.

Rose slipped out of her wet jacket and put it on a hook by the front door. Her tank top slipped off her right shoulder, exposing the slim muscles. Her nipples, like rounded creek pebbles, pushed through the ribbed fabric of her tank. Henry's eyes held her. All of her. He watched a flicker of firelight dance on the wet of her slender collarbone. He saw the goose bumps on her arms. "You're freezing. Let me get you a sweater."

Henry returned a moment later and wrapped his worn cardigan around Rose's shoulder. She breathed in the smell of him, then looked over Henry's shoulder to an easel that was in the corner of the living room. Henry followed her gaze and saw a soft question in her brow.

Rose nodded to the easel. "You paint now?"

Henry laughed. "God, no! I just…" Henry had a hard time finding the words. "I saw it in the window at Thelma's thrift shop and thought maybe if you came by again, you could paint something. A sunset or a heron or…" Henry's words trailed off. "I'm not sure if it's nice or not. But Thelma said it was good and she gave me some paints and paper too."

Rose wrapped her arms around Henry's neck. Her breasts pushed softly into his chest. She felt strong and whole in his arms. She felt like his.

Rose pulled back and looked into Henry's eyes. "It's perfect, Henry. It's all perfect."

Henry looked at her, then snugged his sweater tighter around her body. "Let me make you some tea."

"No, let me do it," Rose replied. "I need to figure out where things are if I'm going to stay here tonight."

Henry felt his heart open as the words settled in. Rose returned from the kitchen a moment later with a kettle, mugs, and tea bags. She put the kettle on the wood stove, then sat down on the couch facing the window. She patted the seat next to her. Henry sat, his knee brushing hers.

"Where do you think it's going?" Rose asked, nodding in the direction of a tugboat motoring down Emerald Pass.

"South," Henry said.

"You're incredibly literal for a songwriter."

Henry thought for a moment. "South into the unknown."

Rose repeated the phrase and added her own alteration. "South into mystery."

"I like that," Henry said.

"Maybe we should write music together."

They sat quietly and watched the boat as it pushed a rolling wake from its bow.

"Two minutes," Henry said. Rose raised an eyebrow. "I used to sit down on the beach when I was a kid and count the seconds until the waves came. A tugboat wave takes 120 seconds to hit the shore. A cargo ship is 115 seconds. It's the submarines that surprise you. They displace so much water." Rose leaned into Henry. "If you're going to know where the tea is, I might as well teach you everything else about living at the cabin. I'd hate to leave any of it in my head before you go."

The kettle whistled from the wood stove, spitting water into a sizzle on the hot plate. Rose stood, reluctantly, and walked to the stove. She poured two cups of tea and walked back to the couch. When she sat down again, Henry wrapped a wool blanket over her shoulders.

Welcome Home

Henry and Rose fell into the comfort of each other as the day wore on. They sat on the couch looking out over the moving world and told stories. Henry told her about the cabin. He told her how, when he was a child, his father caught the kitchen on fire when he forgot about a birthday cake in the oven. He shared the story of when a powerful north wind rolled through the cove and blew down a two-hundred-year-old fir tree. The tree fell through the cabin roof and landed next to Henry's bed. He woke to a mad rush of wind.

"A bough scraped my cheek like a cougar claw." Henry thumbed two light scar lines on his right cheek. "I remember the smell of it. Fresh and green. It was an odd feeling. Like the forest wanted the cabin back. I suppose it's just a matter of time, anyway."

Rose reached up and ran her thumb over the scars on his face, then she shared the story of her own scar. How when she was a little girl she would dance in the woods behind her house. She imagined all the animals of the forest watching as she jumped and spun in the air like an acrobat. Once, she tried a

360 spin and landed it perfectly, but when she stretched up in her finishing pose she hit her head on a tree limb.

"It didn't hurt, but there was lots of blood and I was terribly embarrassed even though it was just me and the squirrels."

Henry laughed, then leaned down and kissed the scar with warm lips. "I knew there was a story there," he said. Heat ran through Rose's body from where his lips touched her skin.

Rose told Henry about her love of color and light. She told him about a moment in Paris when she watched the sun light up the Champs-Elysées so it looked like it was glowing. How it made her cry. How beauty could move her to tears in a moment.

"I feel things deeply. I used to be ashamed of that. But now I love that part of me," she said.

Rose felt Henry's desire for her, but it did not hold eager expectation. A light tension floated between them—suspended—then edged closer by the gravity of inevitability. Henry stood and added a log to the wood stove. Rose felt the loss of him, his absence leaving her wanting. There was love in this man that she had never felt. Something unique that her soul tapped into like a puzzle piece finding its home. Rose did not believe that true love could only be found with one person. Like shifting light, she believed in shades of love. Some were more vivid and moving than others. All of it was warm and worthy of appreciation. But next to Henry, she began to rethink her philosophy. Henry made her feel like the whole world was glowing. Not a wildfire, but a glowing heat that felt steady and sure.

The smell of wood smoke trailed in Henry's wake as he sat back down on the couch. Rose snuggled into him fully for the first time and they melted into each other. Henry inhaled the scent of her. He took her deep into his lungs, making her part of him. Wood smoke, rain, sweat and lavender.

By mid-afternoon, any intrusion from the outside world felt like an assault on something sacred. So, with a heavy heart, Henry mentioned an errand he had to run.

"I hate to say it, but I need to drop off a table at Arthur's for his potluck tonight and I promised my agent that I'd send my new contract by the end of the week. The good news is, we need groceries and I can pick those up while I'm out."

Rose smiled. "An agent? How Hollywood."

"I know, it's all ridiculous, but I promised I'd send him the contract, and I love the work, so the show goes on."

Henry thumbed Rose's knee, stood from the couch, and walked into the bedroom. When he returned, he was wearing black jeans, old cowboy boots, and a faded T-shirt. He leaned down and kissed Rose on her forehead.

"You look like a cowboy."

"I am a bit. I guess."

Rose watched Henry walk out the door and across the porch. He moved fluidly and familiarly. Rose thought about seeing him on the roof: the swing of his hammer, the cabin framed by centuries-old cedar trees. *A picture to paint,* she thought.

She walked to the easel and clamped a piece of paper into place. She looked through the basket of paints and selected a variety of blues. She set them on the table and dabbed at them with her brush. Blue. "Blue, blue," she said to herself as she ran strokes across the top of the page. She tried to match the color of the sky to what she remembered when she first saw Henry. She added some white to the blue and settled on a shade that felt right.

Rose painted as the sun skidded across the sky and the tide emptied from the cove. She felt herself slide into her project. A familiar feeling returned. It was that way when she painted. A sliding into. A bumpy slope at first, then a smooth slip as the art took its hold and washed over her.

By the time the receding tide had exposed the mudflats, Rose had completed a rough outline of the cabin. She stood back and looked at the painting and realized that she was living in the art. Real-life adjacent, as if she were living in something two-dimensional. Something that she could not take with her. Something held in place by a frame. Being with Henry was a floating life, woefully unattached to the world she actually occupied. It was different for him. Henry was able to be with her fully. Without attachment. She was playing house, but how lovely the house was. When she had walked through the brambles at the end of Kingfisher Lane, she had transcended into something that was hers, if only for a moment. She felt the brevity of it, the floating nature of her and Henry, and she decided to indulge in it all. She waited for shame to flood in but felt only the narrow bend of the paintbrush between her fingers.

Henry returned an hour later, groceries in hand. He watched Rose dancing through the window. She had turned up the music and stopped mid-spin when she saw Henry outside the door. She watched him with a coy smile as he fumbled with the bags. It was the first time she'd seen him move with clumsiness and she enjoyed teasing him with her inattention.

When Henry motioned for help, Rose mouthed, "I can't hear you." Finally, she relented and opened the door.

"Thank you!" Henry said with a huff.

"It was the least I could do."

"Indeed it was." Henry bumped her with the bags of groceries and gave her a challenging smile as he walked by.

Henry's relaxed humor was refreshing when compared with her husband's matter-of-fact intensity. Whenever Rose's humor came to life at a party or social gathering, Simon would give her a look and call her silly. Never funny. Always silly. There was something so demeaning in "silly." Simon preferred jokes that weren't masked in nuance. A linear joke with a clear punchline. Everything felt linear with Simon. One thing to the other. Always a plan. Always a destination in mind. It was a very effective way to live but there was no room for the mystique and certainly no dancing across the living room floor with groceries that needed to be put away.

Henry sat the bags on the counter and moved his hips from side to side, then Swazied his way across the room toward Rose as the Rolling Stones played on the stereo.

"You look like a horny chicken!"

"That sounds about right," Henry said.

"My God, Henry, here I was thinking you had some measure of talent."

Henry put his hands on her hips and began moving her across the living room as Rose laughed uncontrollably.

"Make it stop!" Rose screamed as Henry scooped her up in his arms and twirled her in a circle. On the second rotation, he stopped short and set her back down. He was looking over her shoulder at the half-finished painting on the easel. Rose followed his eyes.

"Do you like it? It's been years since I've had time to do anything but sketch."

"Rose!" Henry said. "That is the most beautiful thing I've ever seen."

The rest of the evening melted away like ice on a summer sidewalk. Slant light streamed through windows in the living room as Henry chopped onions and garlic in the kitchen. A pot of water boiled on the stove as spot prawns flipped their tails in a metal bowl.

"In they go!" Henry yelled from the kitchen. Rose heard a splash and the top of the pot slam tight.

"Gah! I hate doing that," Henry said.

"You're such a brute, Henry!"

"I'm not, I swear…it's just that they taste so good."

Rose laughed. The rain fell. *Humor*, she thought. *What an aphrodisiac.*

Vivaldi played on the record player while Rose painted and Henry set the table for dinner. He served boiled shrimp, Caesar salad, and fresh bread. They shared a bottle of chardonnay as they talked about adventure and possibility. They indulged in the idea of traveling together, of waking to the sunrise in Rome, of lying together on a beach in Costa Rica. When the plates were empty, Henry walked into the kitchen and pulled a fresh blackberry crisp out of the oven. He plated two slices and then scooped on a mound of vanilla ice cream.

"When did you make that?"

"Well, I was going to take it to the potluck tonight but it seems I've already improved my company, so…no need for all that." Henry knew Arthur would be sore by his no-show and he was not sure how he would explain the circumstances.

Rose took the plate of dessert and walked across the living room to a box of records that sat on the floor next to the turntable. She fingered through the titles, then pulled out Joni Mitchell.

"I met her once," Henry said as Rose held up the album. "At a songwriter's party in LA. She called me Hank. I loved it."

Rose put the record on the turntable and dropped the needle. "All right, Hank, name that song."

After two notes Henry yelled out. "Easy."

"What is it then?"

Henry slid his chair out from the table and walked to where Rose knelt on the floor. He extended his hand and as he pulled her up, he said, "I'll tell you, but only if you dance with me."

Rose tucked her hair behind her ears. "You drive a hard bargain, Henry."

He pulled her in close, their bodies moving together, as Joni sang. Rose tucked her head under Henry's chin. She could smell the wine on his breath. She felt her heart weaving into his, like an impossible knot fixed tighter with each passing moment.

"'River,'" Henry said.

Henry felt his heart grow and tear and grow again. Proximity made clear the truth that space had questioned. Their souls were meant to be shared. It felt cruel that the world would endow him with such a strong desire for a woman whose life was built elsewhere. *The world is like that, I suppose, doling out love and heartbreak at random. Heartbreak,* he thought. Henry put his hands on Rose's shoulders and stepped back so he could see her.

He looked into her emerald eyes and spoke softly. "There is something in me that you've brought to life. I feel it crashing in on me like a tidal wave. You are the one I've been looking for. I dreamed it."

Rose buried her head in Henry's chest and in his warmth, she found the realization that she could no longer settle for subtle shades of light. She had been lying to herself. Glowing was better than being dimly lit.

Rose put a hand behind Henry's head and drew him close. The kiss was soft and warm. Henry put his hands on Rose's cheeks and held her. He ran his thumbs along her cheekbones. He made a soft sigh as her lips fell from his. The feeling after a sunset. Rose pushed Henry onto the couch. She swung her legs over him and settled on his lap.

She put her hands in his hair and tilted his head toward her. "I could kiss you forever," she said as she leaned forward and found his lips again.

Breathe with her, Henry thought, as he took in the landscape of her lips, committing the taste of her to memory. Then he charted her neck with his lips. Slow kisses behind her ear.

Warm kisses along her neck. Henry took his time discovering the landscape of Rose. She breathed in his scent as she allowed herself to be known. Henry wanted to map every arch and angle of her. A cartographer charting sacred land. The nape of her neck, the curve of her collarbone, the arch of her breasts. With each kiss, Henry drew out the feeling in Rose that she was not only in an adventure, but that she was the adventurer. She was a beautiful discovery within herself.

As their lips found each other, Rose felt Henry's desire between her legs and she edged her hips in response. She ran her hand down to his fly, working each button free. She slid off his lap, kneeled on the floor, and pulled off his pants, discovering him pushing hard against the fabric of his boxers. Rose rested her face on the outside of his boxers, feeling the heat of him on her cheek. She turned her head, and exhaled. Henry breathed in sharp as Rose freed him. She gripped him loosely and trailed her hand down the length of him, following her hand with a light skim of her tongue. Henry slid down on the couch as Rose ran a slow row of kisses to the base of him. She peered up to Henry's face. Each kiss created a reaction of want. She pulled away, holding him in her hand, then slipped him between her lips. Each glide of her lips created a euphoric exhale as she felt desire build through his pulse in her mouth.

Henry reached down and put his hand in Rose's dark hair. He pulled her from him and tilted her chin. The wet of her puckered lips brought a jolt of hunger to his body. Henry felt the calling of his deep, wild self as the thread of restraint slipped through his fingers. He pulled Rose's shirt over her head and she hurriedly unfastened her bra. Then she stood, unbuttoned her pants, and slid them to the floor.

Henry watched the firelight dance off her naked body.

"Don't move. Let me look at you."

Rose smiled and tilted her chin. She felt completely exposed, but the look of desire and warmth in Henry's eyes put her at ease. She stood quietly and let herself be discovered. She could see adoration in Henry's eyes as he took in every single part of her. He leaned forward and gripped her with his hands, taking in the fullness of her hips, then he ran his hands up her stomach and held her breasts in his palms. He slipped his leg between her knees and edged her legs apart. As they opened, Henry leaned forward and breathed in the scent of her. Rose watched a smile work its way across Henry's face. Warmth. Lips. Tongue.

Henry ran a warm hand up from Rose's knee to where she was warm and wet. He leaned forward and bit down on Rose's hip as he slid his fingers over her slick contours. He spoke to her softly, "Be with me."

Rose took a breath and felt the truth of his words. Henry bit down lightly on her hip bone again, adding pressure to the bite as he teased her. Then he rocked her slowly forward with his free hand, slipping the tip of a finger just inside her, his palm pushing lightly on her clit. Rose breathed in deep as he stood and found her mouth with his. He kissed her deep as he arched his fingers forward in a rhythm that matched the sound of the waves. He put his other hand on her heart, feeling the beat on the flat of his palm. He pulled his fingers from inside her and put them in his mouth.

"This is all I want, Rose. Just the taste of you and the sound of the sea." He found her again. Smooth. Rhythmic. Her body rising. "Stay with me. Stay in this moment." Henry kept his hand between her breasts as Rose felt her crescendo rising; each note building until he brought her to a full release, her knees feeling unsteady as she exhaled.

Henry kissed her softly on the lips as Rose's breathing eased, then he wrapped a blanket around her shoulders.

"Let me show you something."

Henry slipped his hand down to hers and led her out onto the front porch. Rose felt the warmth of Henry's hand contrasted with the cool breeze from the north. *Contrast,* Rose thought.

Henry pointed down to the beach. "That's where I saw you. You were skipping a stone. I dreamt about you that night. My song. It filled me. You in the doorway. You on me. The warmth of you."

Henry held Rose from behind. She felt his heat through the blanket. The cool breeze teasing at her exposed skin. She looked down at his hands.

"Wait here. I'll be right back."

Henry wrapped the blanket tightly around Rose and then returned to the living room. Rose leaned on the porch rail and watched the reflection of the cabin on the slow waves. Henry opened the windows above the piano. The scratch of a needle on vinyl, followed by the sound of music, filled the night as Henry walked back to her. Rose smiled and offered him her hand. He pulled her in close. Her face rested on his shoulder. He smelled like soap and woodsmoke. Henry crossed his hands behind Rose's lower back, pulling her torso against his. Her blanket slipped off her shoulder.

When the song ended, Rose ran her thumb along Henry's jawline and then reached up to his lips. Henry took her thumb in his teeth and bit down softly. He pulled her in close and kissed her again. The kiss started soft and sweet. Henry opened himself to the roll of her tongue.

Rose felt Henry's erection grow warm and firm on her belly as he made a low growl. She freed him with a smooth slide of the hand. He bent his head back as she threaded him through the fly of his boxers. The cool air licked at Henry as Rose slid her hand down the length of him. He looked at her with animal intensity. Rose pushed Henry back against the cedar shingles then knelt down, taking him between her lips again. He ran his hand down her neck and took a handful of her hair in his fingers as she worked a slow rhythm with her mouth.

Henry pulled Rose up, took her face in his hands and kissed her deeply. He put one hand behind her neck and ran his other hand up the inside of her left thigh. Rose moved her torso in search of more pressure as Henry pushed her hard against the cabin wall, holding her tight. The cool air blew over her naked body as he kissed her neck. He pulled back and looked into Rose's eyes as he positioned her right leg to the side. She arched her back, opening herself to him as he slid smoothly inside her. He felt her tighten around him as he filled her, one breath at a time. He began a steady, slow motion with his hips. Rose felt her body rising as he spoke to her softly.

"It's you. I've found you." He pushed her shoulders back with his body, gripped her hands and pushed them above her head, holding them against the cabin as he took her. Urgent and full. He lost his restraint as he filled her with powerful thrusts. Rose's breath quickened and she angled her hips forward, catching the pressure of his glide. She pulled her hands from his grip and wrapped her arms around his neck, then leaned back and looked at the desire in his eyes while her muscles clenched in a humming deep release.

Henry slowed then stilled. He held her for a moment, then pulled away, leaving Rose with the feeling that part of her was being lost as Henry stepped back and picked up the blanket. He wrapped it around Rose's shoulders once more. He led her across the porch to the outside shower and let the water come up to heat as he held her in the moonlight. With his desire abated, he looked at her objectively. The arch of her shoulders, the line of her clavicle, the full round of her breasts, the thin scar on her abdomen. She was the art and the artist.

He tested the temperature of the water, slipped the blanket from around Rose's shoulders and motioned for her to step inside the shower. Henry walked back into the house and put two towels above the wood stove to warm as Rose bathed in the hot water. She watched him in the moonlight as he walked through the cabin, feeling the desire to have him close. When he returned, Rose wrapped her arms around him and pulled him in tight. Henry kissed her deeply as the water ran over them both. He lathered his hands, turned her, and ran soap over her back.

As Henry's hands rounded her hips, he felt himself responding to her body again. The speed of his recovery surprised him. Sensing his desire, Rose reached back and laced her fingers around Henry's neck then stood on her tiptoes. She let go of his neck then leaned forward offering herself to him. Henry took himself in his hand and found her as she pushed back into him. He wrapped a hand around Rose's waist and brought her closer. She breathed deep as he filled her.

"I am yours, Henry."

Rose felt him pulse inside her as her body climbed again. Henry took her selfishly, reaching his climax quickly and powerfully. Her nails dug into the cedar siding as she found her release, her body buzzing. Henry slowed then pulled himself from her. Spent. He turned her to face him and wrapped his arms around her. Rose smiled up at him, then buried her head under his chin, forming a single sculpture of the two of them.

Memoryscape
(Wednesday)

Henry woke the next morning, the image of Rose in his dream as real as the woman lying next to him. The morning sun filtered through the windows and cast her dark hair in soft light. Henry was struck with the deep ache of impending loss.

Whenever Henry felt unsure or lonely, he would lean into those feelings as deeply as possible to see if he could push through to the other side. He often found that going deep into an emotion brought him relief–a realization that he was safe and alive. *She's worth the heartbreak*, he thought to himself as he rolled to an elbow, working to push his feelings through to the other side. He watched her sleep. He did not find the other side.

Henry studied Rose's lines and curves as she slept. He memorized the constellation of freckles on her neck and shoulder. One small freckle an inch below her right ear. One small freckle just above her right collarbone. One small freckle at the crest of her left breast. He watched the breast freckle rise and fall in time with her breathing. Wanting to capture the moment in song, Henry rolled from bed quietly and walked to the piano.

> I saw you there
> Moonlight in your hair
> Right in front of me
> By the rolling sea
>
> I found you then
> In my dream that night
> You held on to me
> Just like the morning light

Rose woke to the sound of Henry playing the piano. A soft melody. The same one she'd heard as she descended the trail to the cabin the day before. She smiled at the music as she swung her legs to the floor and walked naked to the windows on the north side of the room. She looked out over the beach and watched the rain fall softly on the water. Gray clouds hung low in the sky, holding the cabin in a pillow of soft light. She found a throw blanket on the chair next to the window and wrapped it around her body, taking refuge from the chill of the cabin as she walked to the small bathroom. She took inventory of

Henry's simple life. Toothbrush, washcloth, soap from the farmers market. Bathtub inside and shower outside.

Simple, she thought. *I like simple.*

Rose washed her face and looked in the mirror. Her skin glowed. *This is me. Circumstances don't shape us*, she thought, *they just reveal our true heart, and my true heart is in love with Henry David James. How terribly inconvenient.* Rose followed the sound of music into the living room. The fire in the wood stove popped and hissed as she walked toward Henry. *Fir*, she thought. A steaming mug sat on the hearth. Henry looked up from the piano and smiled. He stopped singing but kept playing the melody.

"Good morning," Rose said.

Henry fixed her with his eyes. "You are radiant in the morning light."

"What song are you playing?"

Henry looked down at the keys. "It's a love song." He nodded to the fire. "There's a cup of coffee just above the woodstove. I don't know how you take it, but I put a bloop of whipped cream in there."

"A bloop. That's perfect," Rose said as she crossed the living room floor and retrieved the mug off the mantel. "What time is it?"

Henry looked outside to see how far the tide had run up the beach. "Looks like eight-ish."

Rose's pulse quickened. Breakfast was being served at the Island House. She imagined Gail and Bob exchanging glances over her empty chair. Her anxious thoughts were chased away when she heard Henry singing.

>You're my western sky
>My northern star
>My wings that fly
>My there you are

Rose smiled at the last line. "Did you write that?"
Henry looked out the window. "You did."
Rose sat down on the couch, took a sip of coffee, closed her eyes, and smiled. She heard the sound of a chair moving and Henry's footsteps coming toward her. She opened her eyes when Henry took her face in his hands. She hesitated, then fell into the moment and reached her hands up, held his forearms, and pulled his lips to hers. The kiss held them both, floating like the clouds over Emerald Pass. Then all sound quieted. The waves–gone. The wind–gone. The thousand sounds of the wild world–gone. He held her eyes and pulled his lips from hers. He slid his hand into hers and pulled her up from the couch. He held her. He let her scent fill his body. Then they walked back to the bedroom hand in hand and made love to the sound of Oyster Creek.

Yellow Leaves

Rose walked to the footbridge over Oyster Creek and listened to the water. She wanted to take in as much of the place as she could before she left for Spokane. She saw a flash of silver.

"Welcome home," she said into the creek.

The smell of bacon and coffee called her back to the cabin. As Henry prepared breakfast, he cast sideways glances at Rose's backpack by the front door as if it were a moving truck in the driveway. Rose caught Henry's gaze as she walked in the front door.

"Damn you," she said. Henry squinted his eyes. "Damn you and this damn perfect little cabin."

Rose walked to Henry and put her arms around his neck. "I feel like I'm leaving home to go home, Henry. I feel caught between belonging and responsibility."

Henry smiled and folded her into his arms. "I'll always be here, Rose. I've gone years not knowing what you feel like. And now that I've felt it, now that I've felt you, I'm not going anywhere." Henry took a breath and fixed his eyes on hers. "But I don't want little bits of you. I want all of you. Every single bit.

I can live with the hope that we may be with each other one day, but not with the agony of getting you a bit at a time."

Rose looked out the window as a tear pooled on her lower eyelid. "But I like your bits."

"I like your bits too."

After breakfast, Henry walked heavy-footed to the front door, shouldered Rose's pack, and handed her the maple hiking stick.

"Spokane by dinner means catching the 10:30 a.m. ferry." Rose looked at the clock on the wall just as the minute hand clicked into place. Half past nine.

They walked up the trail to Kingfisher Lane as if they were descending into dense water, each footstep a fathom, each switchback a league. Rose watched her pack rise and fall on Henry's shoulder. When they came to the lane, Rose took Henry's hand and they walked down the road in silence, gravel crunching, leaves falling. Rose let go of Henry's hand just before they reached the path through the brambles and jumped to a yellow maple leaf.

"Just the yellow leaves," Rose said as she took a giant step from one leaf to the next. Henry smiled and leaped. "We have to hold hands, though!"

They swerved down the lane, Rose holding the hiking stick in one hand and Henry's fingers in the other as they jumped from yellow leaf to yellow leaf.

Rose looked at Henry when they reached the end of the lane. "Maybe I could stay? Maybe this is where I need to be." They both sat with the words, knowing they were not true.

"The place is right. We are right. The time is not. Go. I'll be here. If this is home, we will find our way back to each other."

Rose squeezed Henry's hand, then reached up and kissed him softly. He felt the fullness of her lips as an alder sapling brushed at his leg. He tried to take it all in. He wanted to remember everything. Her hair in the morning light, the warmth of her lips … but it was impossible, and he resigned himself to just feel. Feel her next to him. Feel her lips on his.

A feather floated from the canopy and settled itself on Rose's hair as they stood next to the bramble-lined path to the Island House. Henry's eyes widened. He picked up the feather and spun it slowly in his fingers. He took Rose's backpack off his shoulder and stuck the feather into a patch that had come loose at a corner.

"I'll want that back one day," Henry said. Rose nodded through tears as she shouldered her pack. She put her hand to his cheek, then turned and walked down the trail.

Henry watched her disappear through the brambles. He stood looking into the void, then closed his eyes and listened for the sound of a car door or an engine. All he heard was the wind filtering through branches above.

He walked back to the cabin in slow motion, stopping on the footbridge over Oyster Creek to watch a salmon jump from one pool to the next. When he arrived at the cabin, he stood in the doorway and surveyed the empty room. He crossed the floor to the piano, put his fingers on the keys, and brought her back note by note as the wind from the open windows ran over his face.

>   I saw you there
>   Moonlight in your hair
>   Right in front of me
>   By the rolling sea
>
>   I found you then
>   In my dream that night
>   You held on to me
>   Just like the morning light
>
>   I felt you there
>   Standing next to me
>   Like water rushing home
>   To the sea

Grant Gosch											Kingfisher Lane

You're my wild Rose
You're my Ocean Blue
You're the one I chose
I'm in love with you

You're my western sky
My northern star
My wings that fly
My there you are

Henry

Alder Island, Today

Oscar is whining now, his high-pitched anxiety whine that lets all creatures within earshot know that he's come upon the most important thing in the world. Most likely it's a stick stuck to a tree or a dog-mouth-sized stone buried in mud. I can't help but appreciate his excitement. He is passionate about what he wants. I respect that. I know he won't stop whining until I break off the stick or excavate the rock from the mud. I could make him figure it out on his own, the natural-consequence approach to dog ownership, but I'm a sucker for Oscar and he knows it.

Oscar came into my life soon after Rose left it. He was a welcome addition to the cabin and kept my mind from folding in on itself in quiet moments. He was always there with a nose on my knee or a scratch at the door. Just enough of an intrusion to bring me away from my thoughts.

I've met a few women on the island over the years and Arthur did his best to set me up with a variety of old friends, lonely tourists, and even his sister. None of those flames burned bright and he gave up on the endeavor a few years back.

"What the hell is wrong with you, Henry? I'm bringing you diamonds and you're tossing them in the water!"

"Just dim lights in the fog," I would say.

Twice I indulged in the warmth of a woman since I last saw Rose. Once with an old friend who came to visit; the other was a woman who owns the bookstore on the island. We connected after a book reading one night. I helped her clean the store and finish off the wine. We lost ourselves in each other between the poetry and mystery sections but the romance was short-lived. She wanted more than I had to give.

Both encounters left me feeling false and empty and I resigned myself to living a pleasant, quiet life writing songs as Oscar thudded his tail on the wood floor next to the piano. I live each day with the sweet, aching memories of Rose. And despite the heartbreak, I am happy to know the love I felt. It's been a good life. A true life.

Rose

Alder Island, Today

Rose pulled into the gravel drive at the Island House and smiled at the sight of Feather Beard's VW bus. Rust had claimed the shroud around the wheels. New layers of bumper stickers filled the side panels representing elections and social causes that had sparked Bob's passions over the past twelve years. The van had become a historical representation of strongly held values.

The front door of the house creaked open and Bob and Gail leaned on each other as they greeted Rose with the same large smiles she grew to love during her short time on the island all those years ago.

"Welcome back, Wild Rose! God damn, you are even more beautiful than last time we saw you!"

Gail stomped on Bob's foot and started down the stairs to greet Rose. Her body swayed more heavily as she walked and she leaned on a cane made from madrone. Gail reached up and put a hand on Rose's face.

"You look radiant. You look alive. My goodness, dear, you are beautiful."

"I feel beautiful," Rose said.

"Well, get your things, darling. We have you back in The Barnacle. You will find that not much has changed here other than the effects of gravity." Gail nodded down to her belly.

Rose gave Gail a warm hug and felt all the comfort of the island in the innkeeper's pillowed bosom.

Rose organized her belongings in the little cottage, then returned to her car for the hiking stick Henry had made for her. She felt the weight of it in her hands. She thought of all the times she had held the stick over the years.

With each bramble she cleared, she thought back over the past twelve years. She thought of the times she'd wanted Henry to come for her. Moments where she would have given anything to be whisked away. He never came. Instead, she leaned into herself. She discovered that home lived within her. That no one was coming to rescue her. That she had the power to rescue herself.

She thought about the freedom she felt when she opened the letter proclaiming the divorce was final. She thought about the pride she felt when the twins, and finally Alex, headed off to college. She thought about the patches she'd added to her backpack the previous fall when she traveled through Brazil, Patagonia, and Iceland.

When the trail opened up onto Kingfisher Lane, she felt light on her feet. She walked up the road and stopped short as a spaniel mutt rounded the bend in the road and began to bark at her. She startled, then followed the dog's eyes to her hiking stick. She raised the stick. The dog sat, scampered its front paws, and wagged its nub tail. Its tongue hung loose from the side of its mouth. She moved the stick from hand to hand as the dog whined. *Silly dog*, she thought.

Henry

I round the bend in the road, the whining getting louder. When my eyes find Oscar, he is crouched like a sphinx, wagging his tail and shifting his hind legs, testing the ground for purchase.

A woman with dark hair, peppered with gray, is looking down at him, her expression changing from concern to amusement when she realizes Oscar's longing is not for her neck but for the stick in her hand. She moves the stick to the right and taps it on the ground. Oscar jumps right. She moves the stick to the left. Oscar jumps left. She raises the stick out to the side and Oscar sits, his long, curly-haired flop ears folded at comical angles. I watch a slow smile cross her face as she realizes that she holds everything in the world that he wants.

When she looks up, I see the small scar on her forehead. I speak her name. Soft, like the wind. The stick drops. The world quiets. I look for a yellow leaf that I can jump to. A leaf that would bring me closer to her. Rose runs to me. I catch her when she jumps. Her legs wrap around my waist, and as I hold her, I say the only words that come to mind.

"Welcome home."

WILD ROSE

I saw you there
Moonlight in your hair
Right in front of me
By the rolling sea

I found you then
In my dream that night
You held on to me
Just like the morning light

I felt you there
Standing next to me
Like water rushing home
To the sea

You're my wild Rose
You're my Ocean Blue
You're the one I chose
I'm in love with you

Grant Gosch — Kingfisher Lane

You're my western sky
My northern star
My wings that fly
My there you are

I like you there
Next to me
Walking through
The cedar trees

The way you looked
On the beach that night
The way you felt
When I held you right

You took my heart
I don't want it back
I didn't know
I could love like that

(Bridge)
Somehow I knew
I'd be right here next to you
My dream come true

Grant Gosch   Kingfisher Lane

You're my wild Rose
You're my Ocean Blue
You're the one I chose
I'm in love with you

You're my western sky
My northern star
My wings that fly
My there you are

You're my wild Rose
You're my wild Rose
You're my wild Rose

The End

For the *Kingfisher Lane* epilogue and performance of the "Wild Rose" song featured in this book, visit Grant's website:

www.grantgosch.com

Acknowledgements

This book would never have come to life without the support of a community of wonderful people, and as usual, most of them are women. I'll try to mention them here, but I will undoubtedly leave a few out. Please feel free to lambaste me through email if I have forgotten you. It won't happen again. I swear…

    Where to start? Kristin, thank you for all the time, phone calls, and happy hours that helped bring this project to life. It would have died on the vine without your thoughts and copyediting. Kyra, I am SO glad I found you; I should say, I'm happy Lenna found you and then connected us (Thank you, Lenna). Your thoughts and feedback were crucial in making this book streamlined. You are fantastic. Speaking of fantastic, Stella! The cover you painted for this book. Come on. You. So good. You brought Henry's cabin and the Salish sea to life with passion, heart, and talent. Thank you. Mom, thank you for your example of an adventurous, strong woman. I owe my dreamer's spirit and love of the Pacific Northwest to you. Ann, you have always improved my work; thank you for proofreading and believing in the book. Your compliments are some of the best to receive. Jon, thank you for the cover layout. You got that talent, brother. I'm glad to have you on the team.

Thank you to my beta readers for taking the time to provide me with detailed feedback, insights, and encouragement. You Rock. Thank you for telling me what's up and down.

Thank you to each of you on my book launch team for helping me bring *Kingfisher Lane* to the world. Keep an eye out for your bookmark in the mail.

Thank you to my wife, Sarah, and my two children for dealing with the ups and downs of having a husband and dad who hangs out in a shack and writes love stories. I hope your friends don't make fun of you at school.

Most of all, thank you to those who have taken the time to read this book. Your thoughts and reviews mean a lot to me. Good or bad, please leave a review before moving on to your next journey between the pages.

Much love to you all,

Grant

For the *Kingfisher Lane* epilogue and performance of the "Wild Rose" song featured in this book, visit Grant's website:

www.grantgosch.com

Keep in touch

Join Grant's newsletter: eepurl.com/hU9Ewn

Follow Grant on Instagram: www.instagram.com/grantgosch/

Visit Grant's Website: www.grantgosch.com

Printed in Great Britain
by Amazon